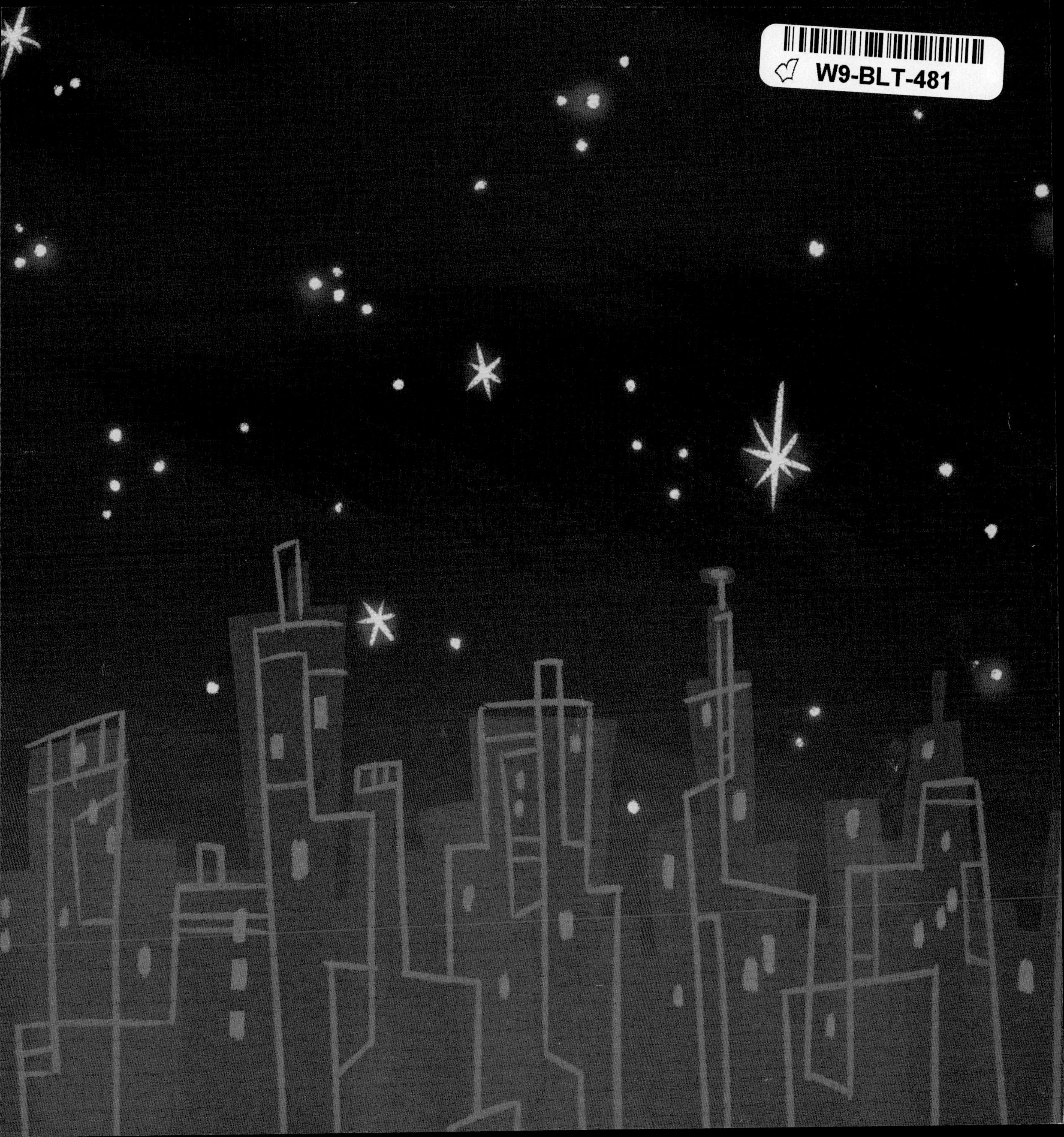

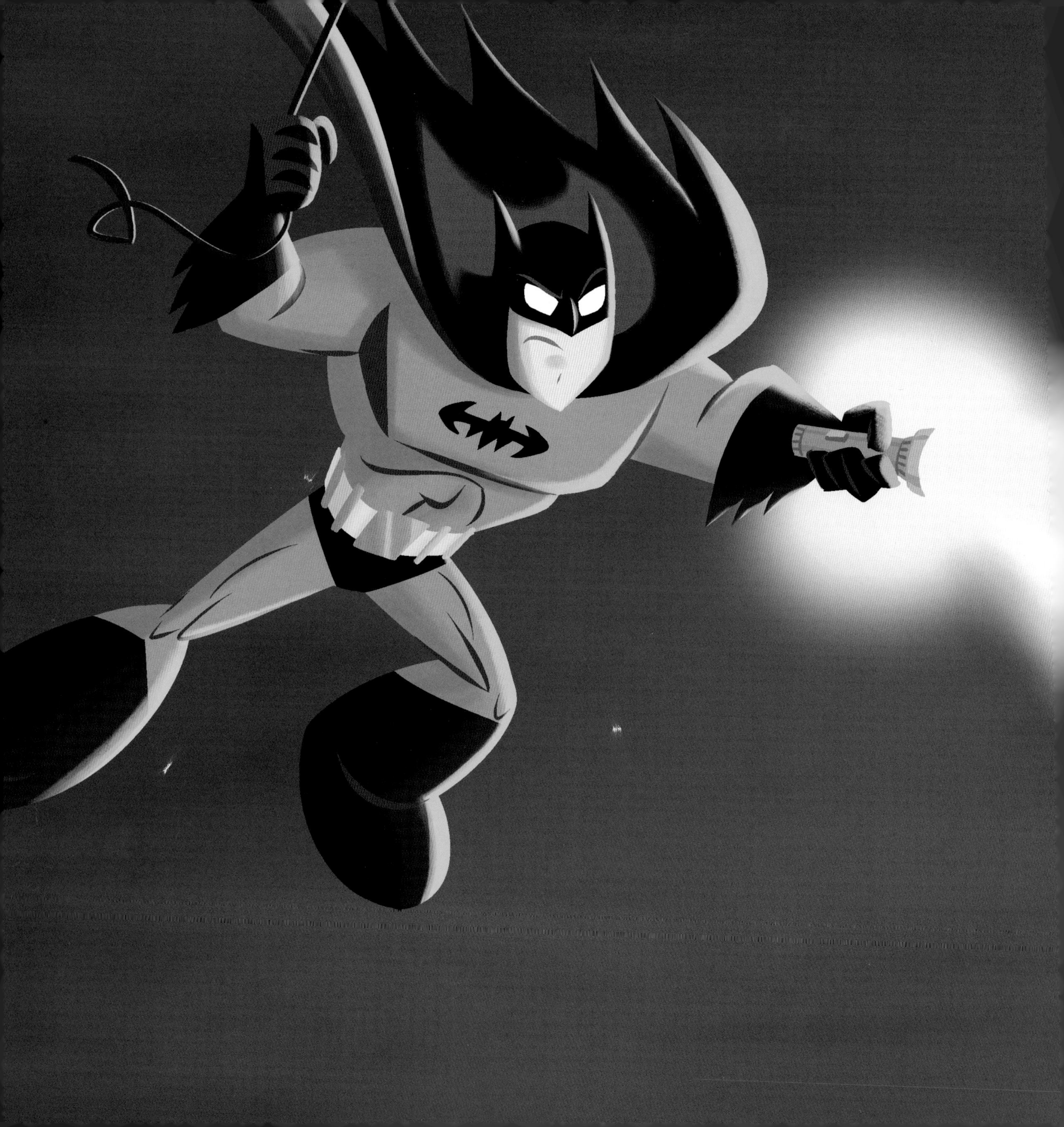

This book belongs to _____LIAM S._____

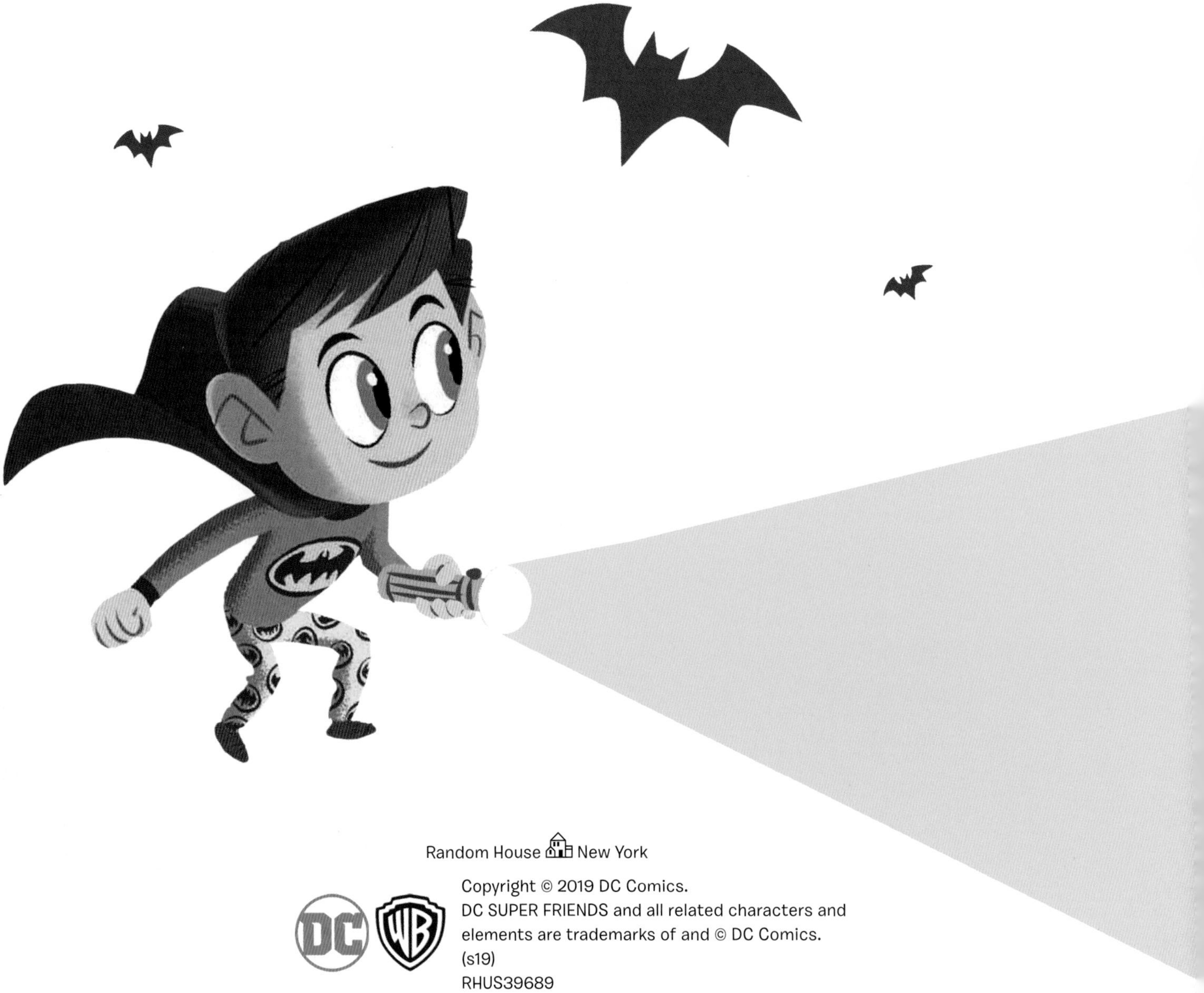

Random House New York


Random House and the colophon are registered trademarks of Penguin Random House LLC.
rhcbooks.com
ISBN 978-1-5247-6915-4 (trade) – ISBN 978-1-5247-6916-1 (ebook)
MANUFACTURED IN CHINA
10 9 8 7 6 5 4

# BE BRAVE LIKE BATMAN!

**By Laura Hitchcock · Illustrated by Ethen Beavers**

Batman created by Bob Kane with Bill Finger

The editors would like to thank Robert Seaver, MD, for his assistance in the preparation of this book.

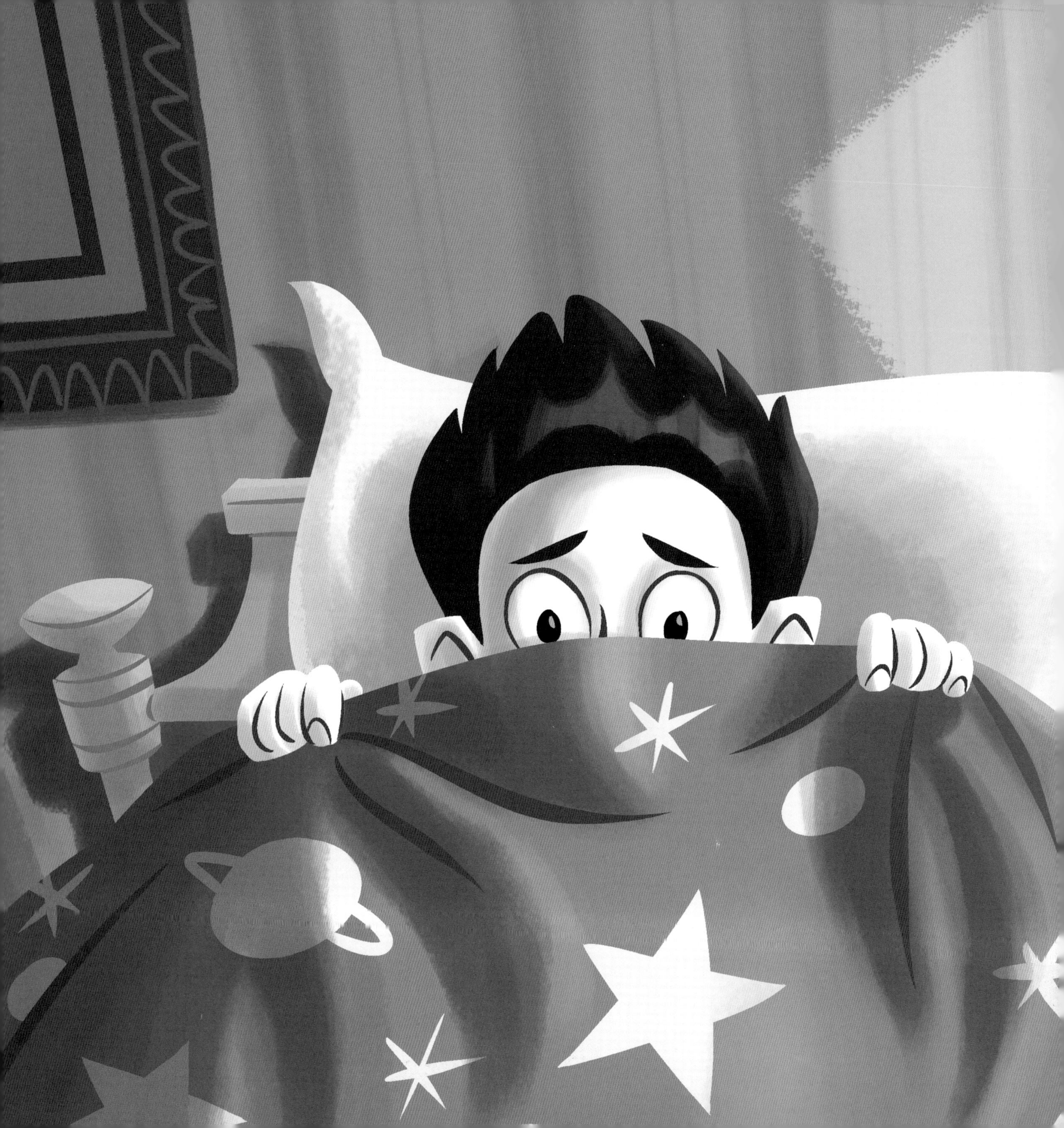

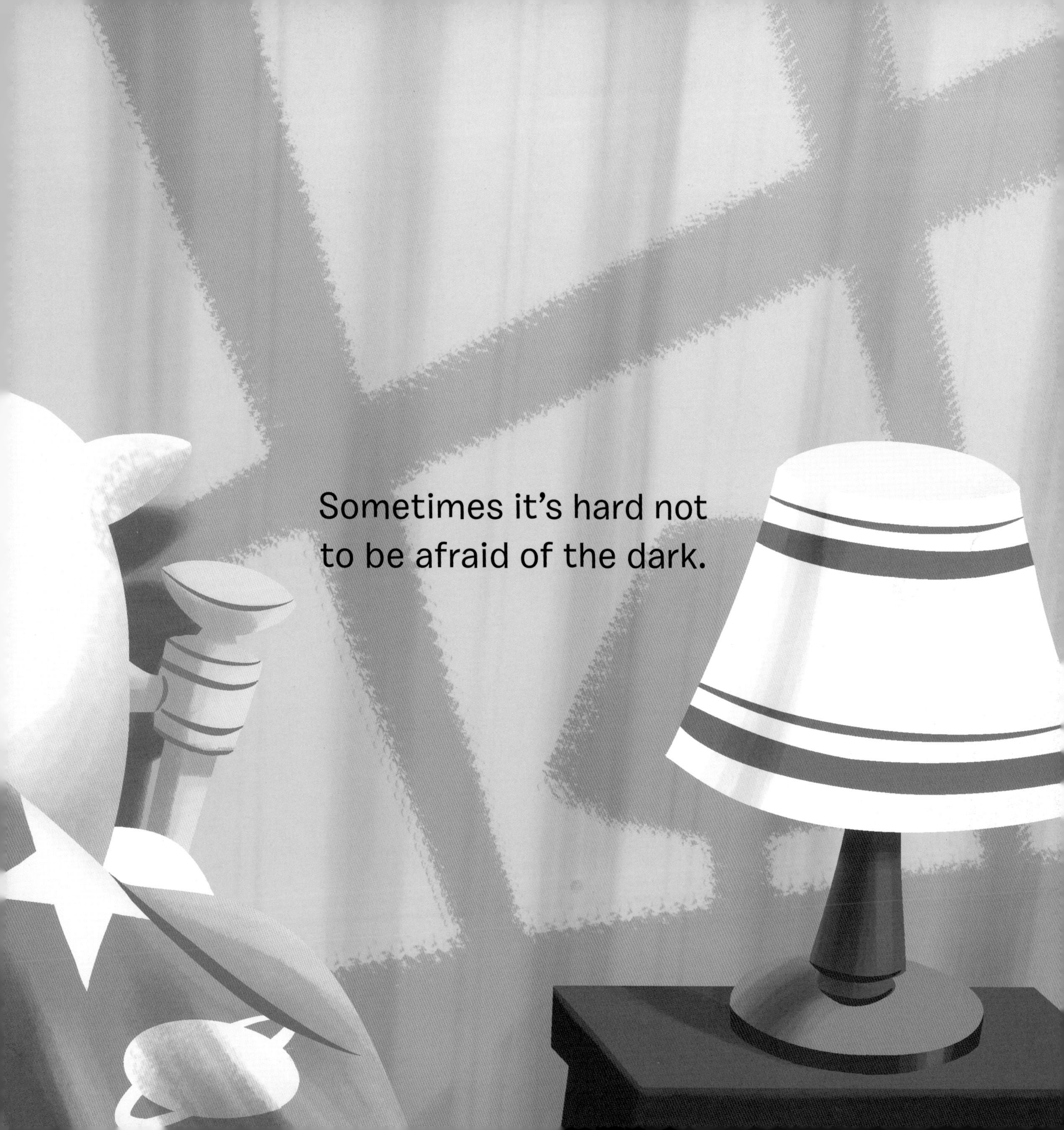

Sometimes it's hard not
to be afraid of the dark.

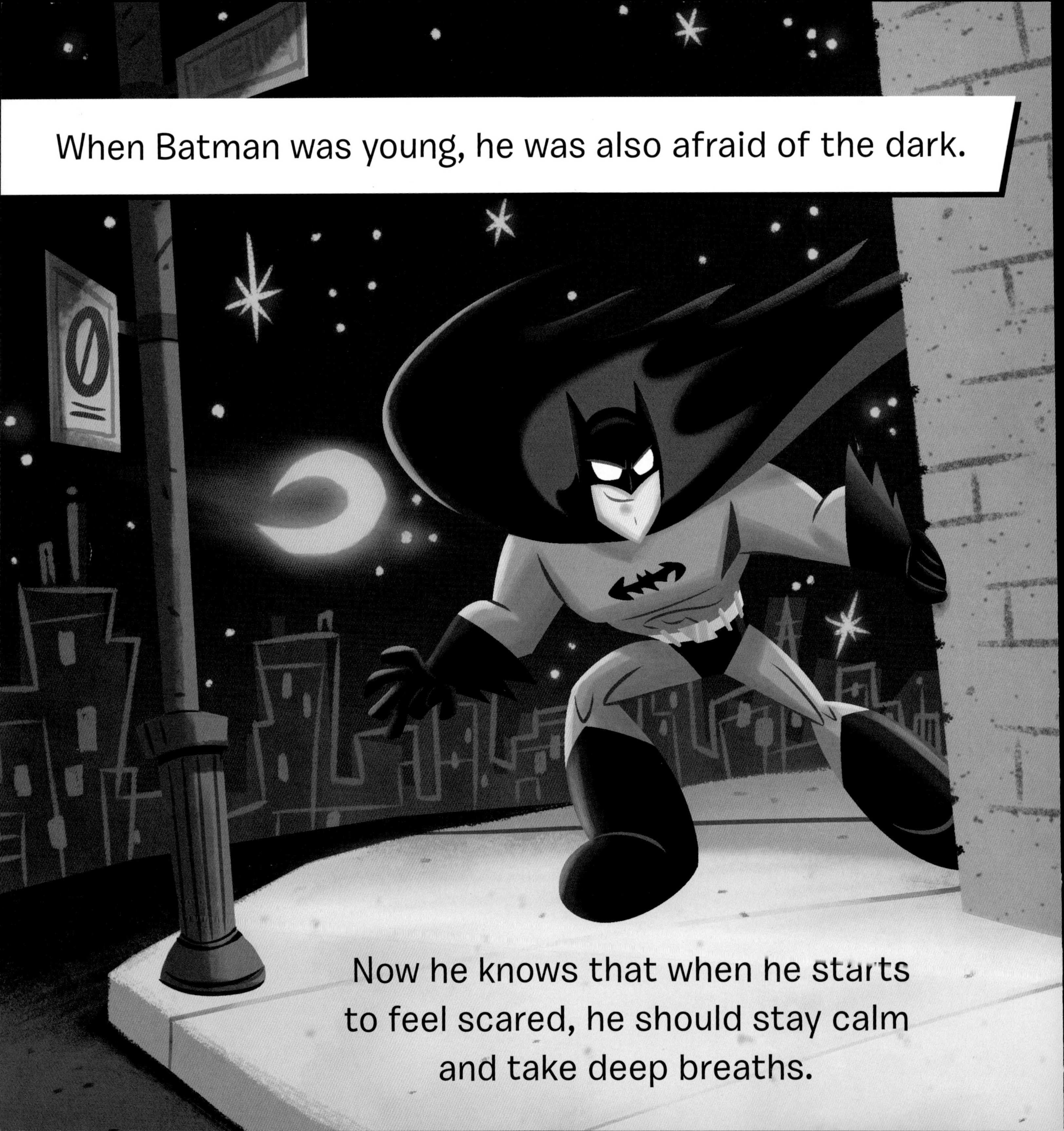

When Batman was young, he was also afraid of the dark.

Now he knows that when he starts to feel scared, he should stay calm and take deep breaths.

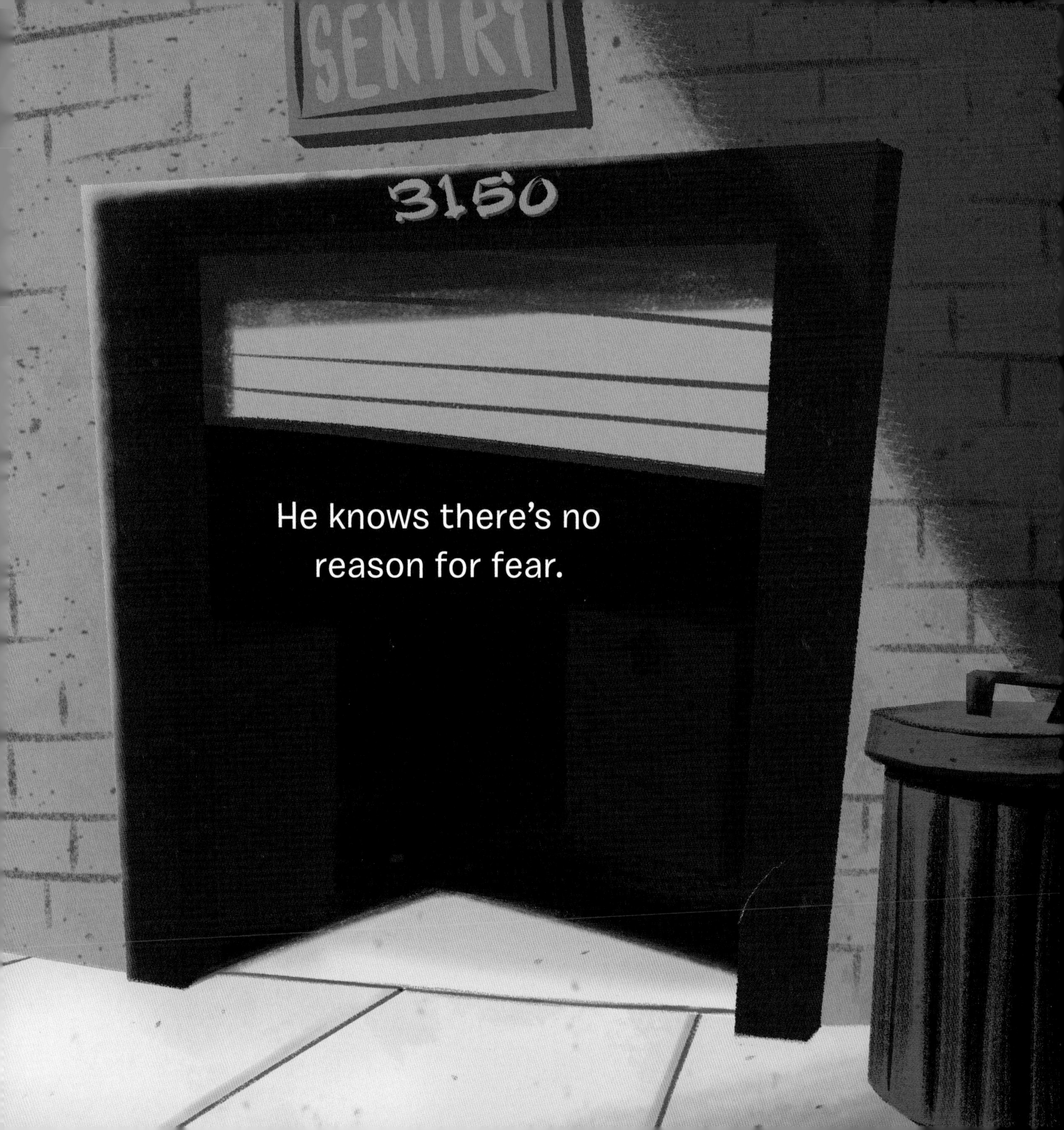
3150

He knows there's no
reason for fear.

You know how to stay calm
and take deep breaths, too.

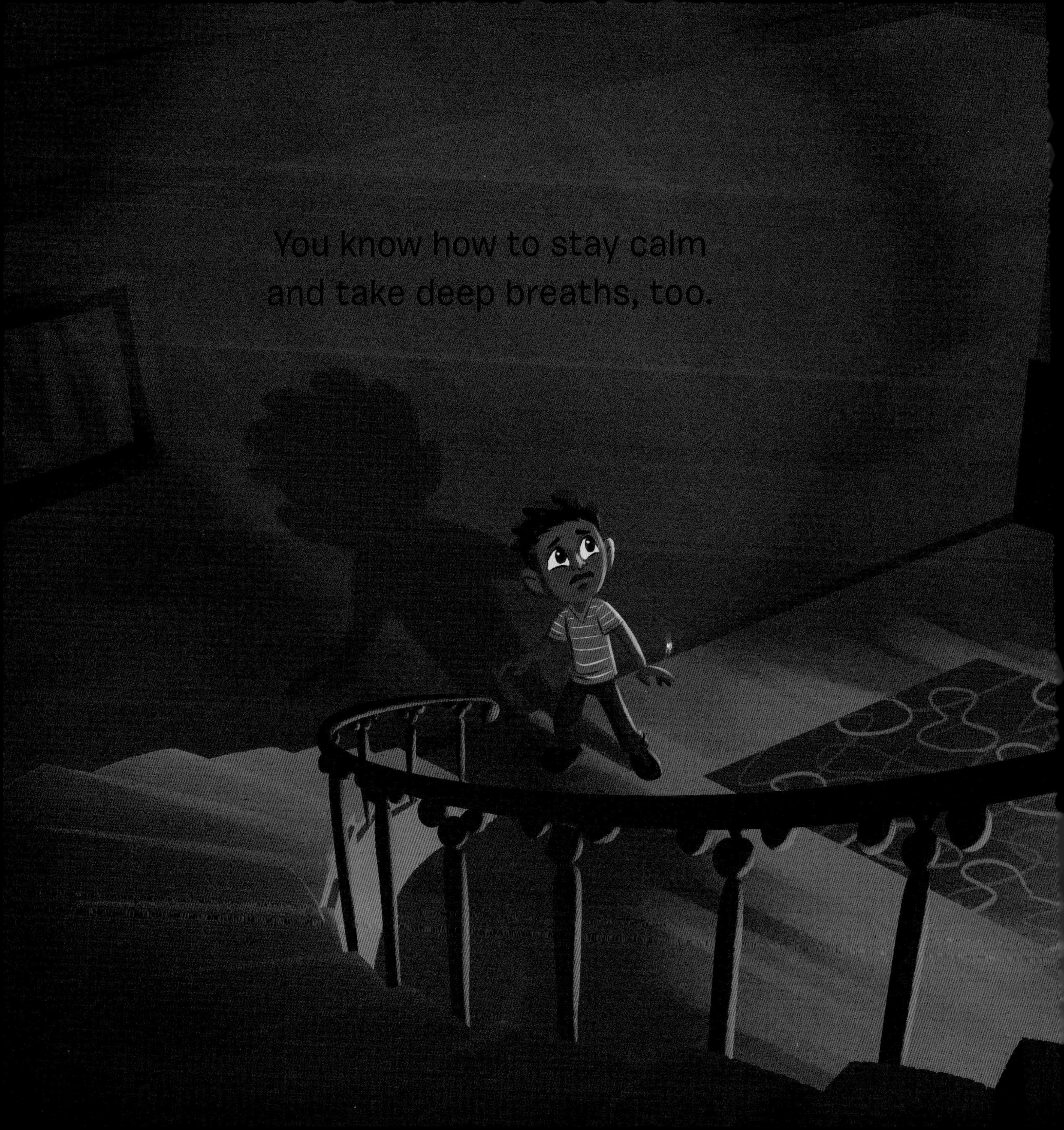

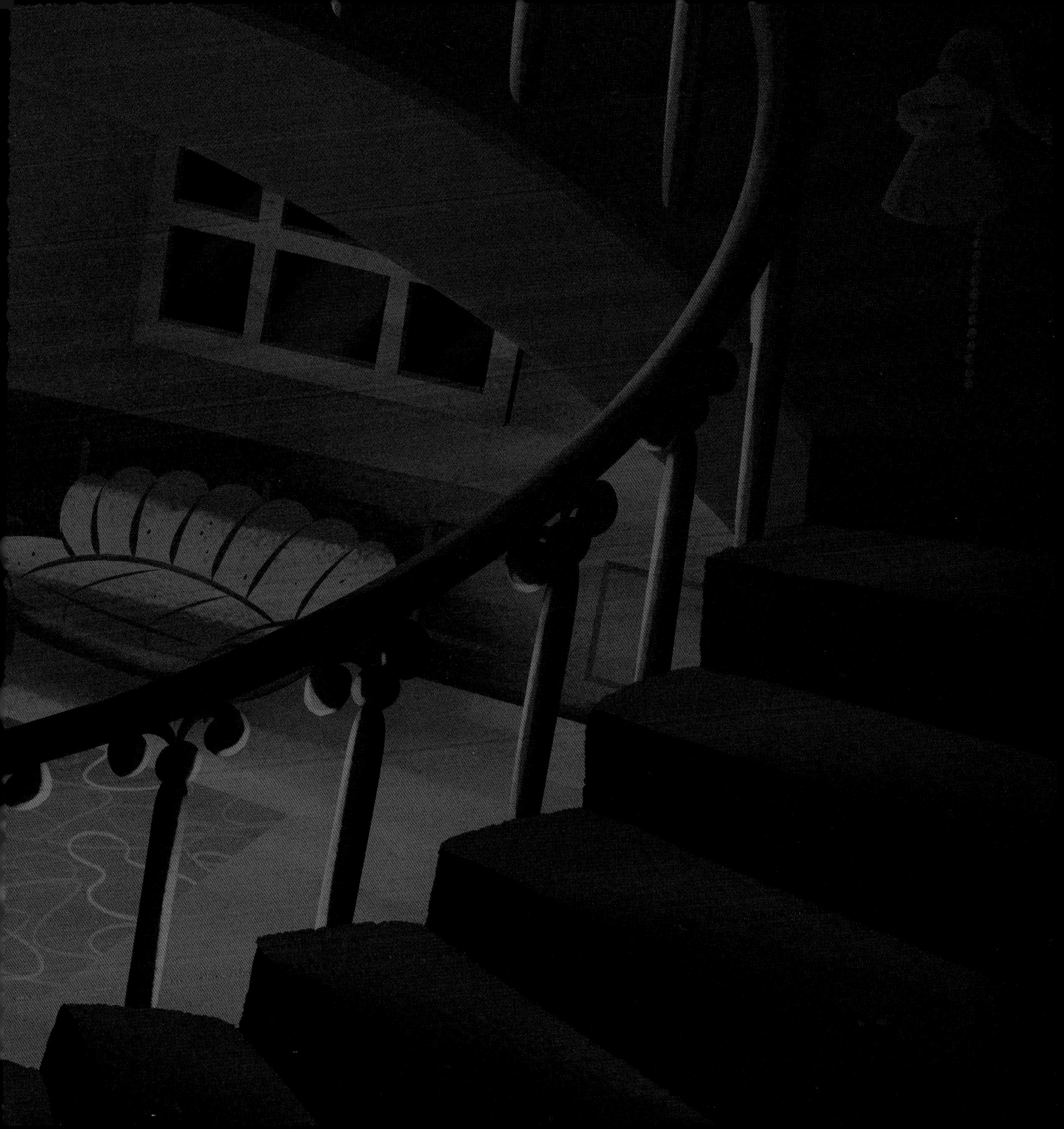

Be brave . . . like Batman!
Nighttime doesn't have to be scary.

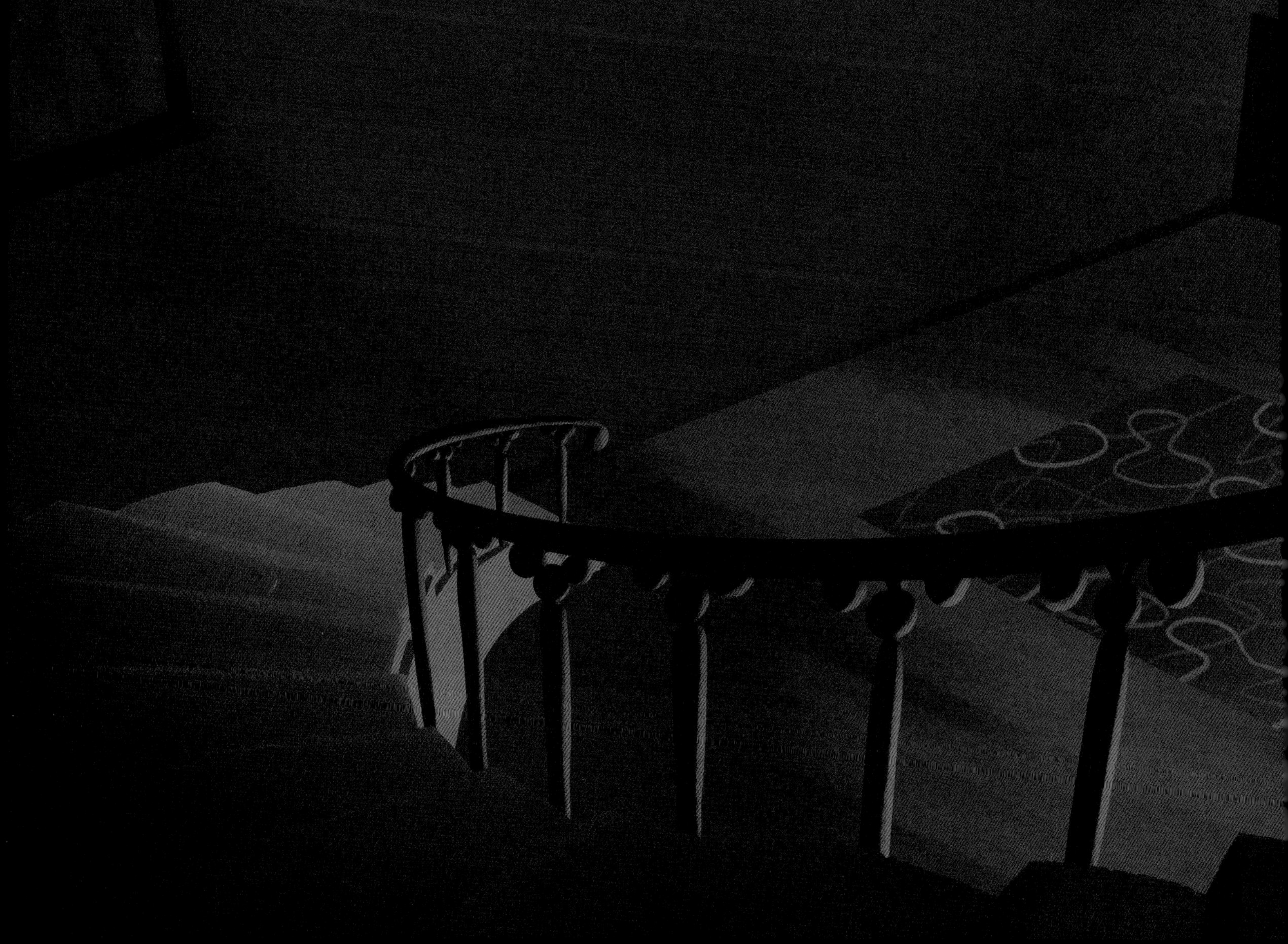

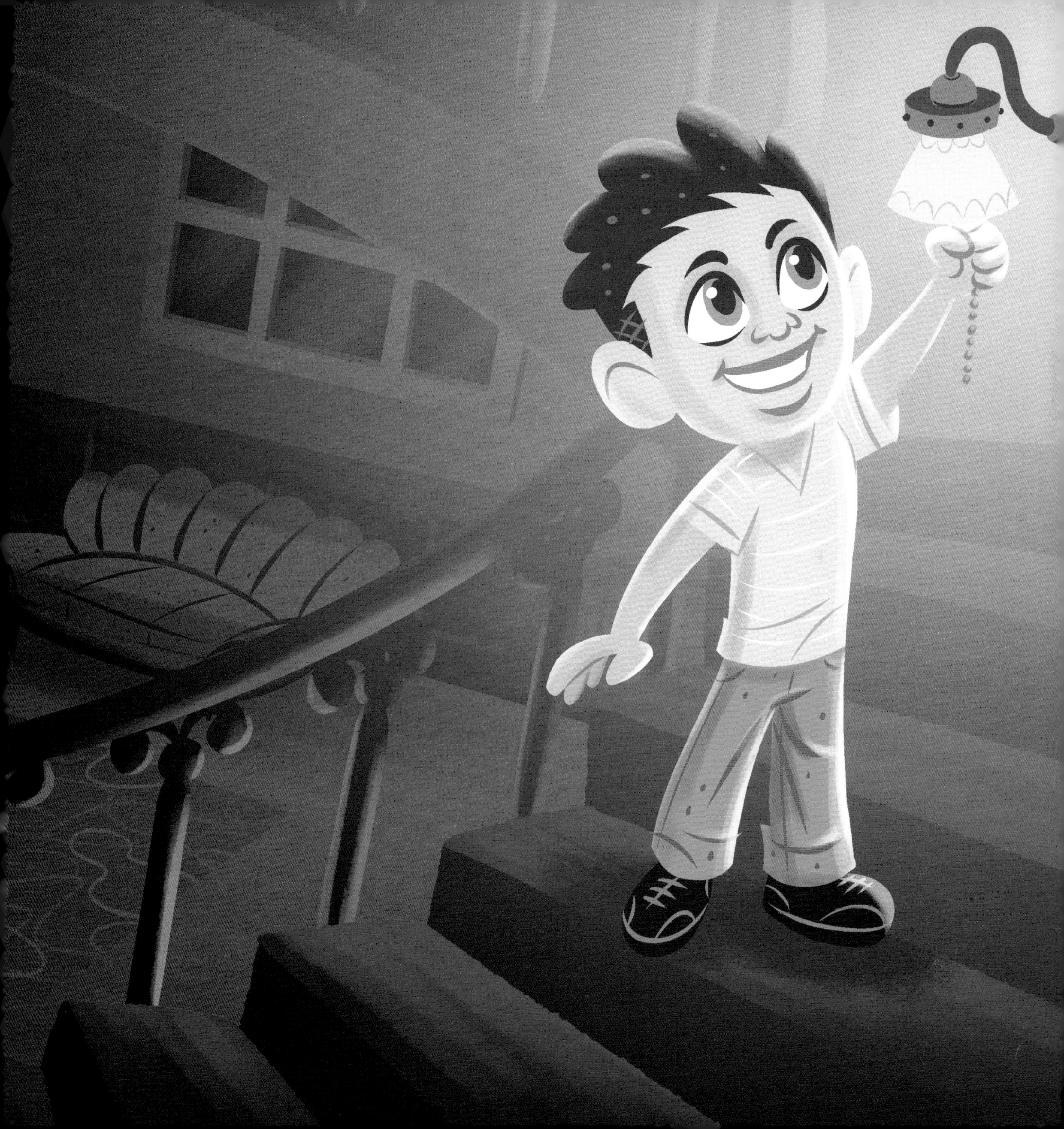

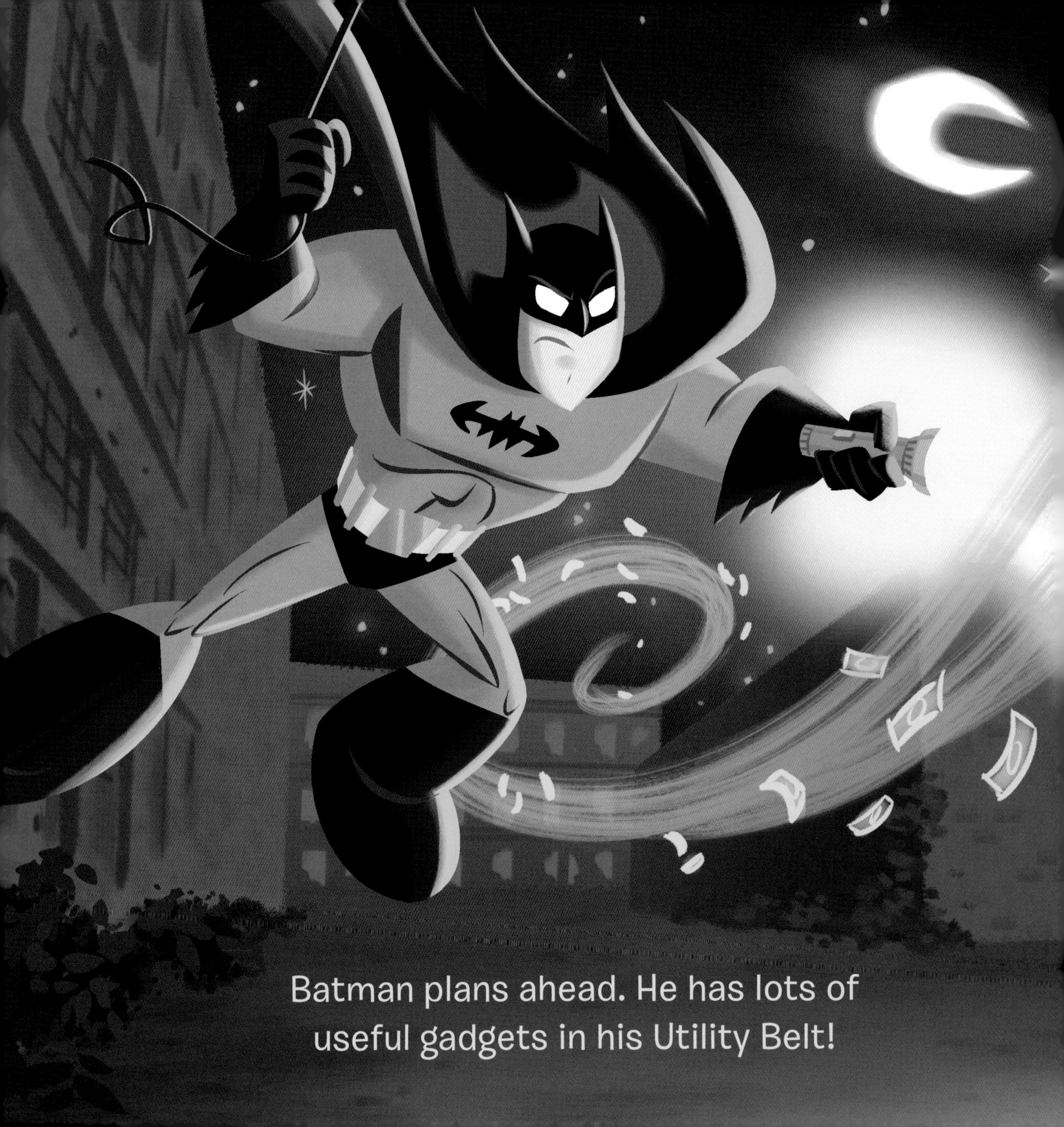

Batman plans ahead. He has lots of useful gadgets in his Utility Belt!

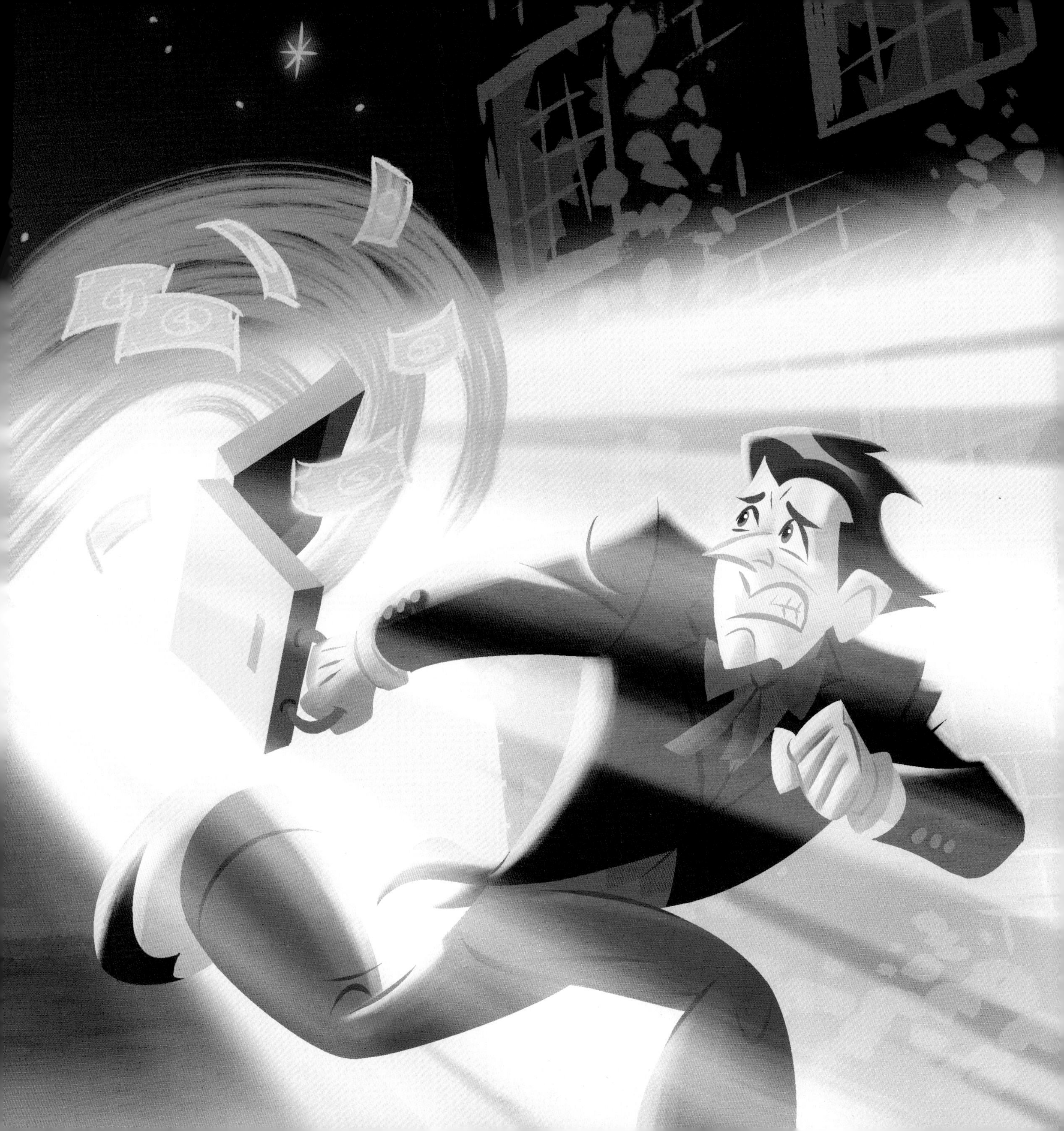

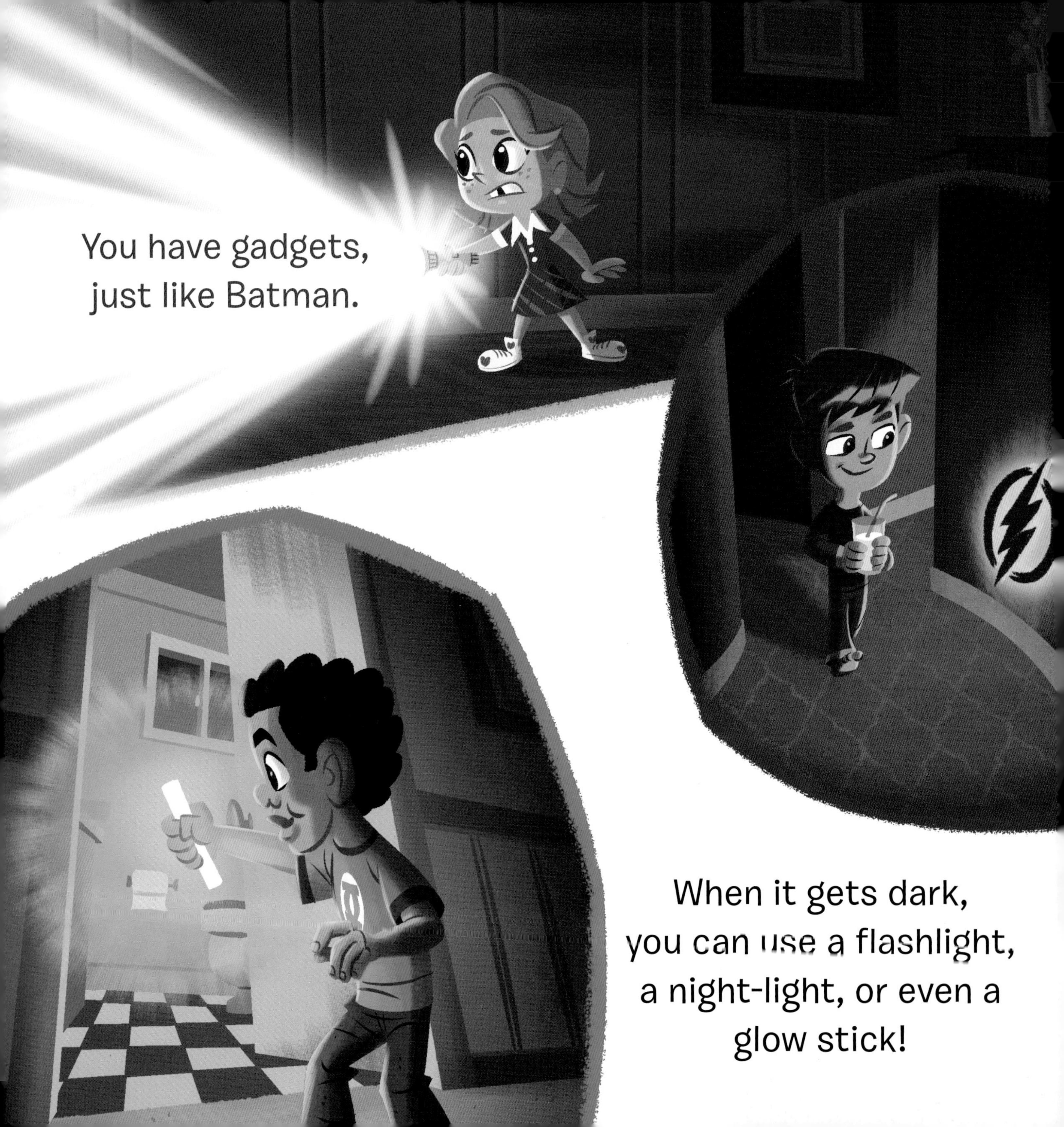

You have gadgets,
just like Batman.

When it gets dark,
you can use a flashlight,
a night-light, or even a
glow stick!

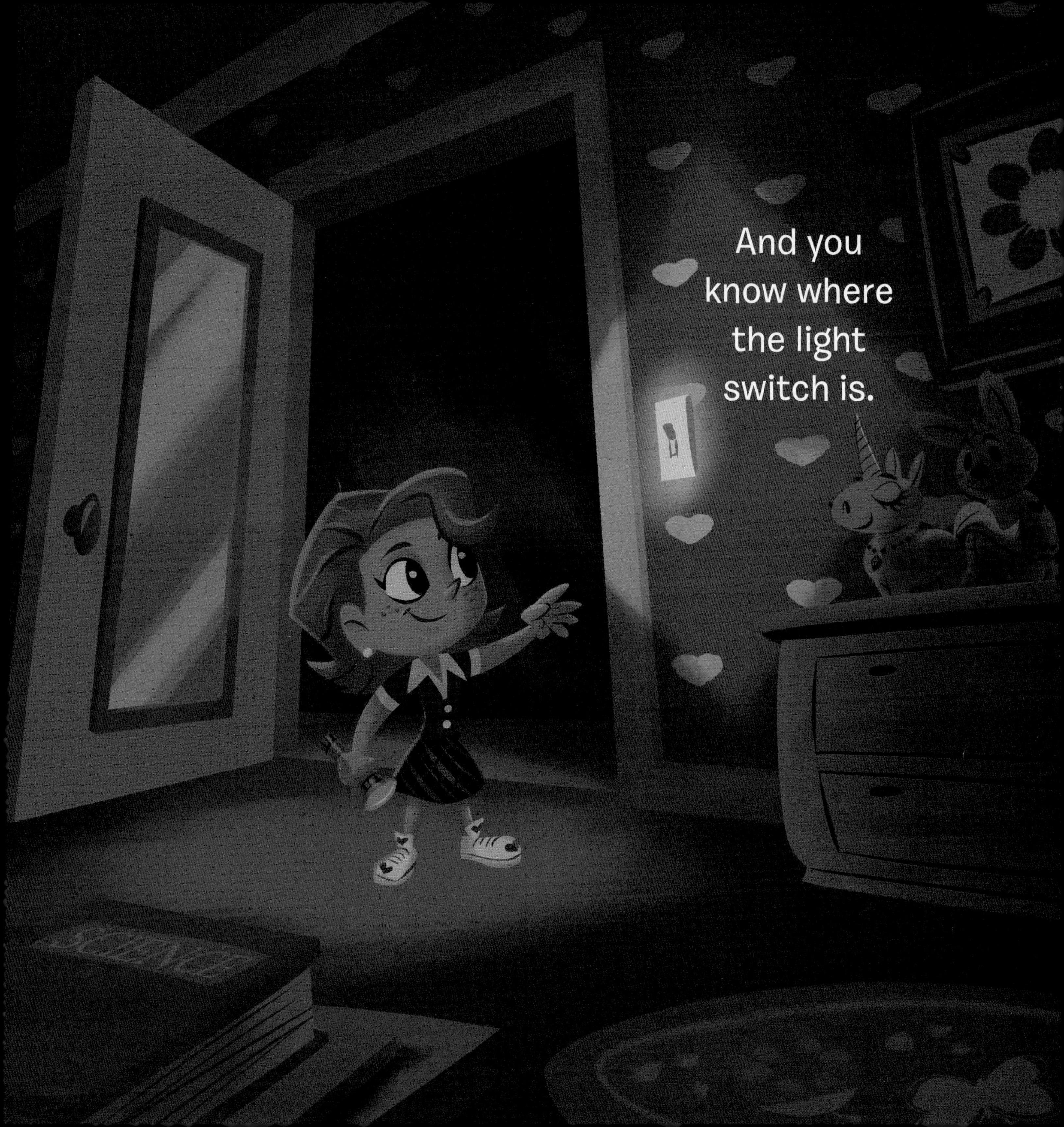
SCIENCE

And you
know where
the light
switch is.

Batman knows it's important to have help.
Robin is always ready to lend a hand.

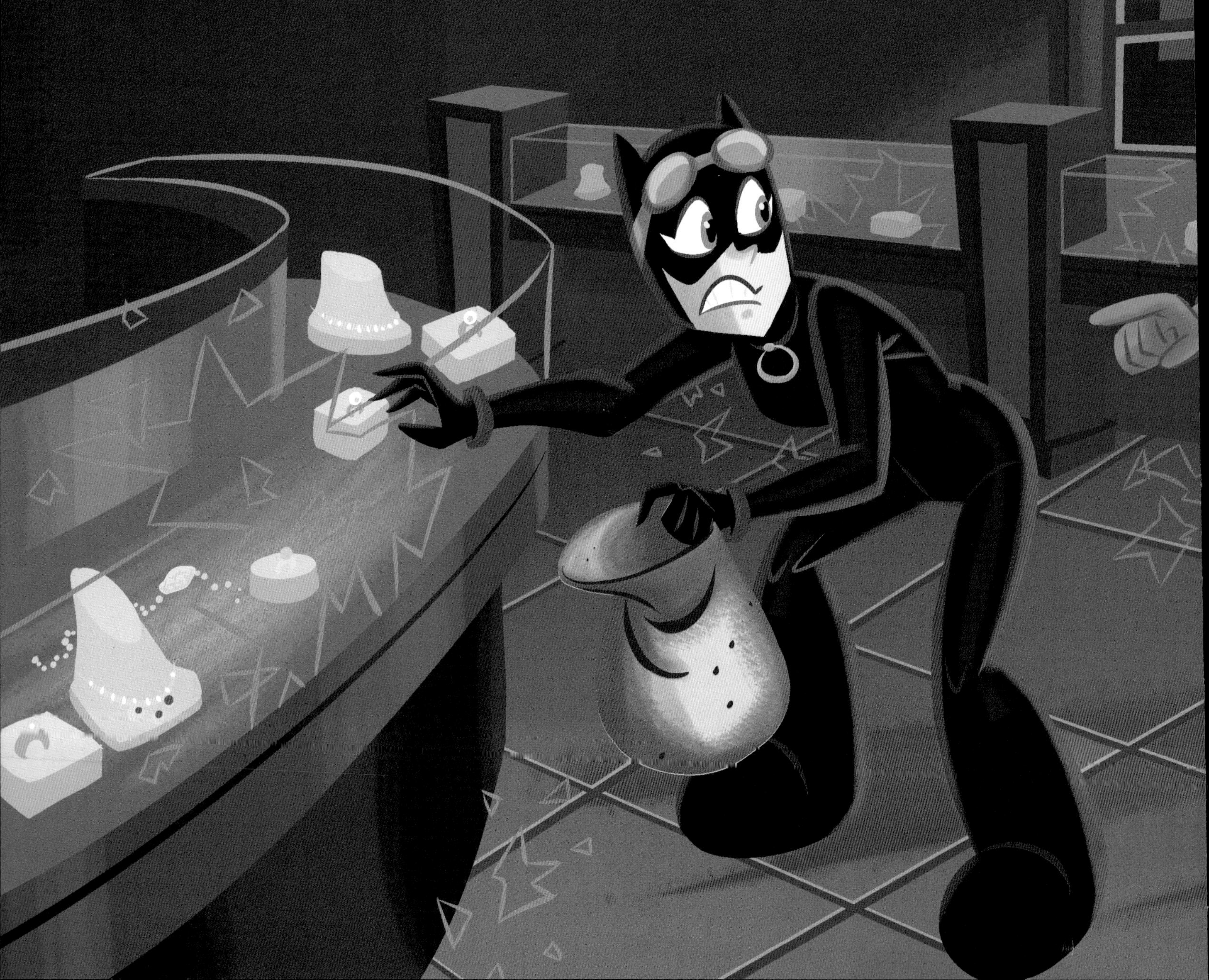

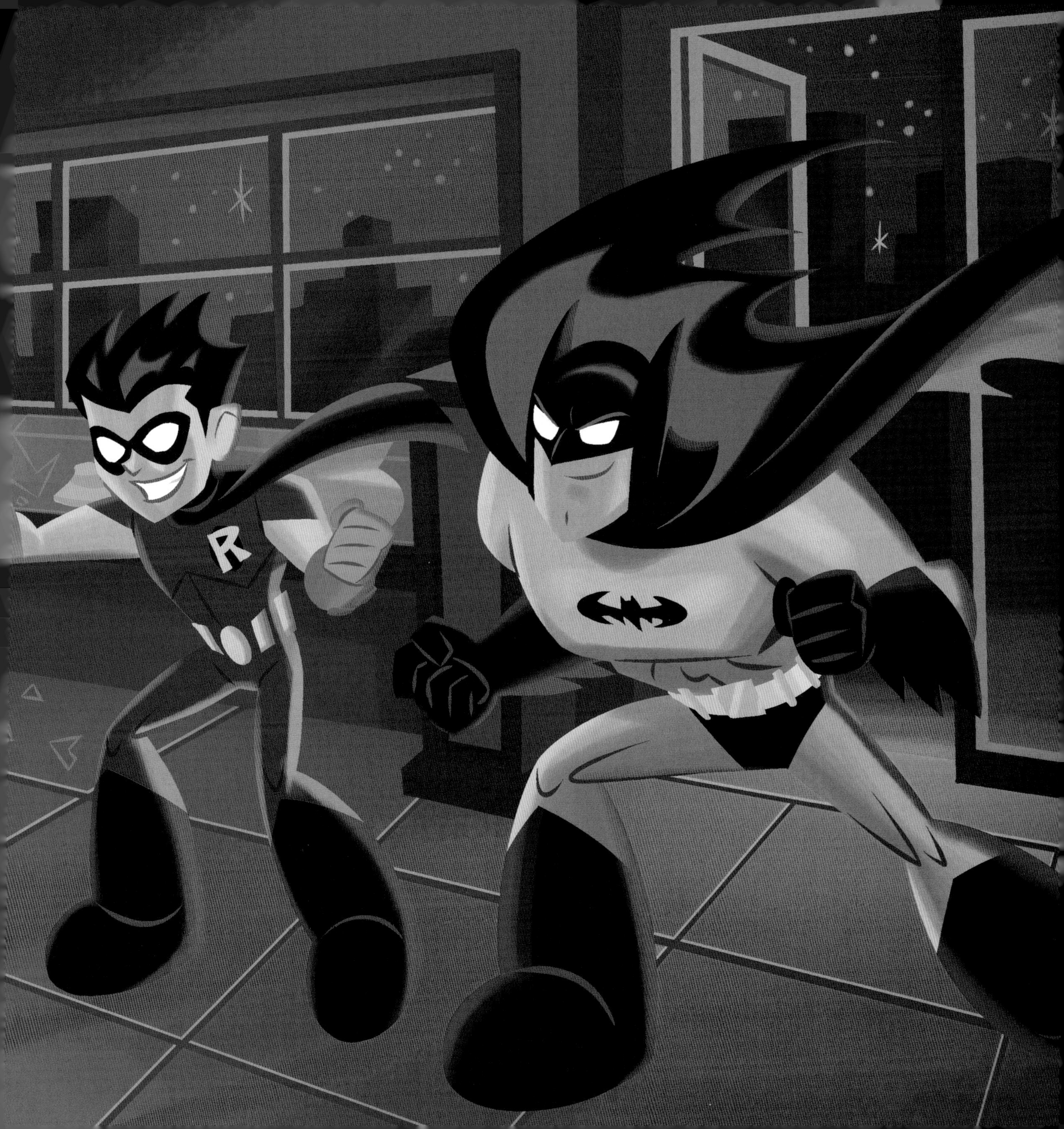

If you're nervous about going somewhere dark on your own, like the garage . . .

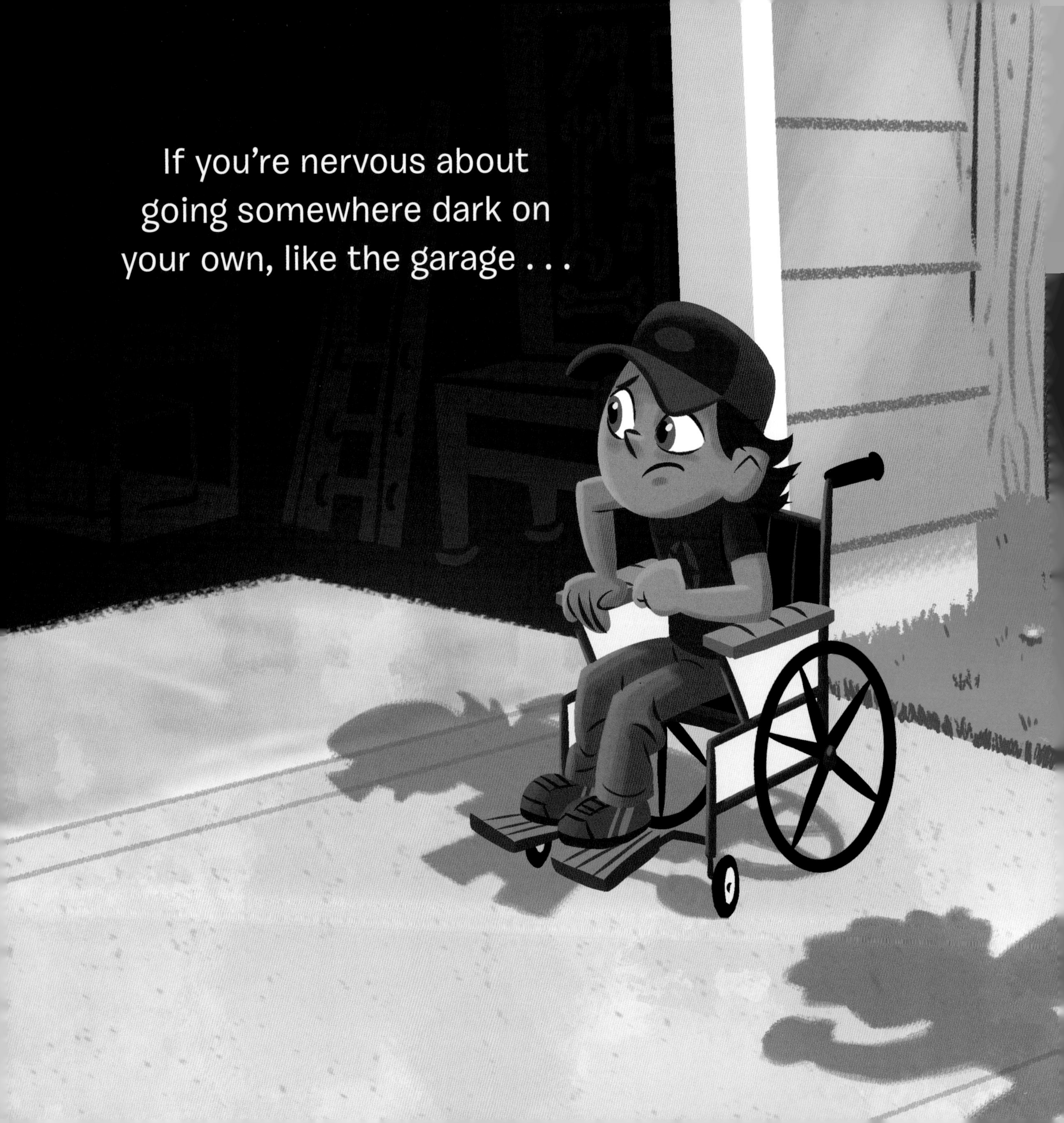

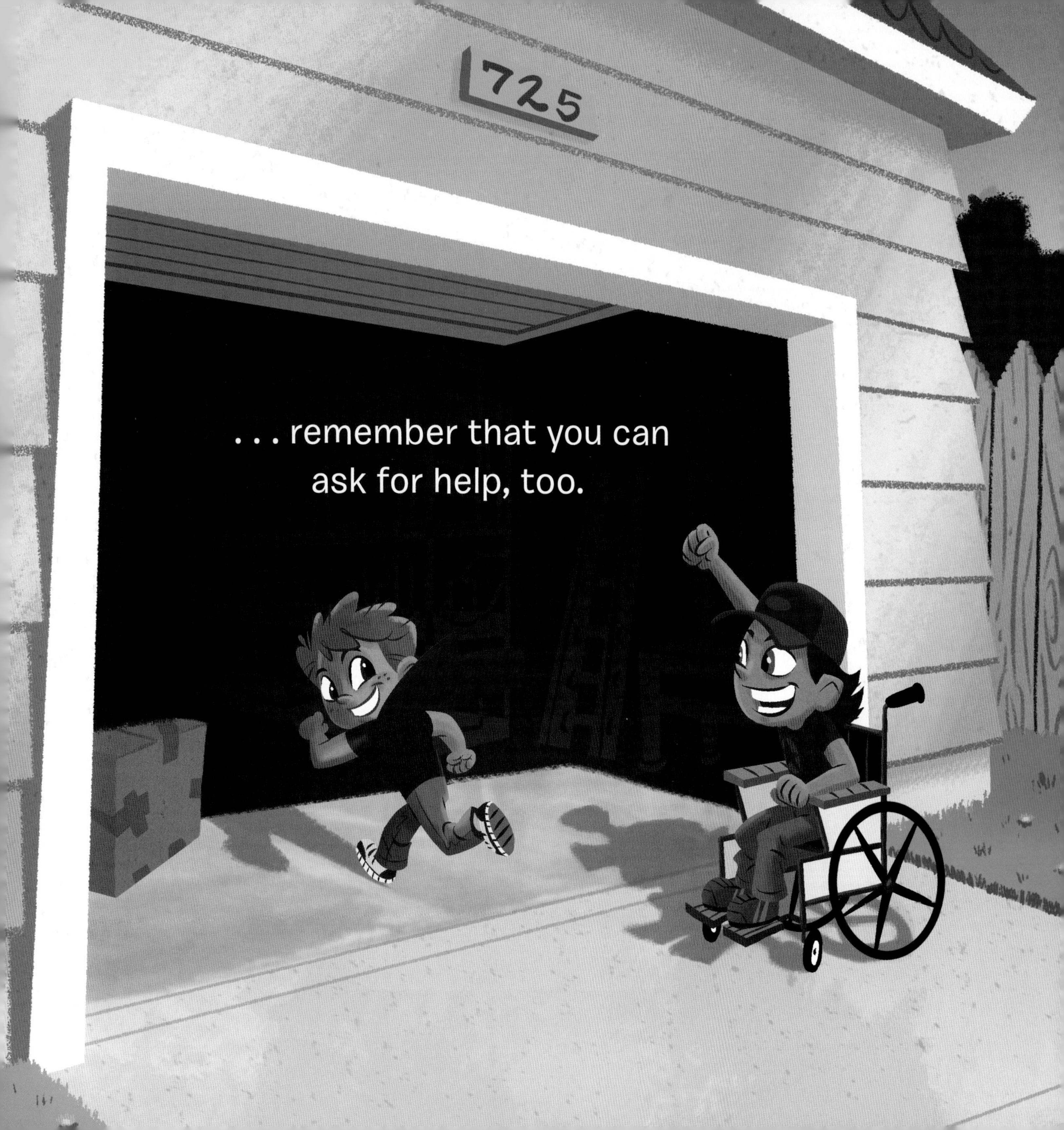
725

. . . remember that you can
ask for help, too.

A brother, sister, or friend
can help find and carry stuff!

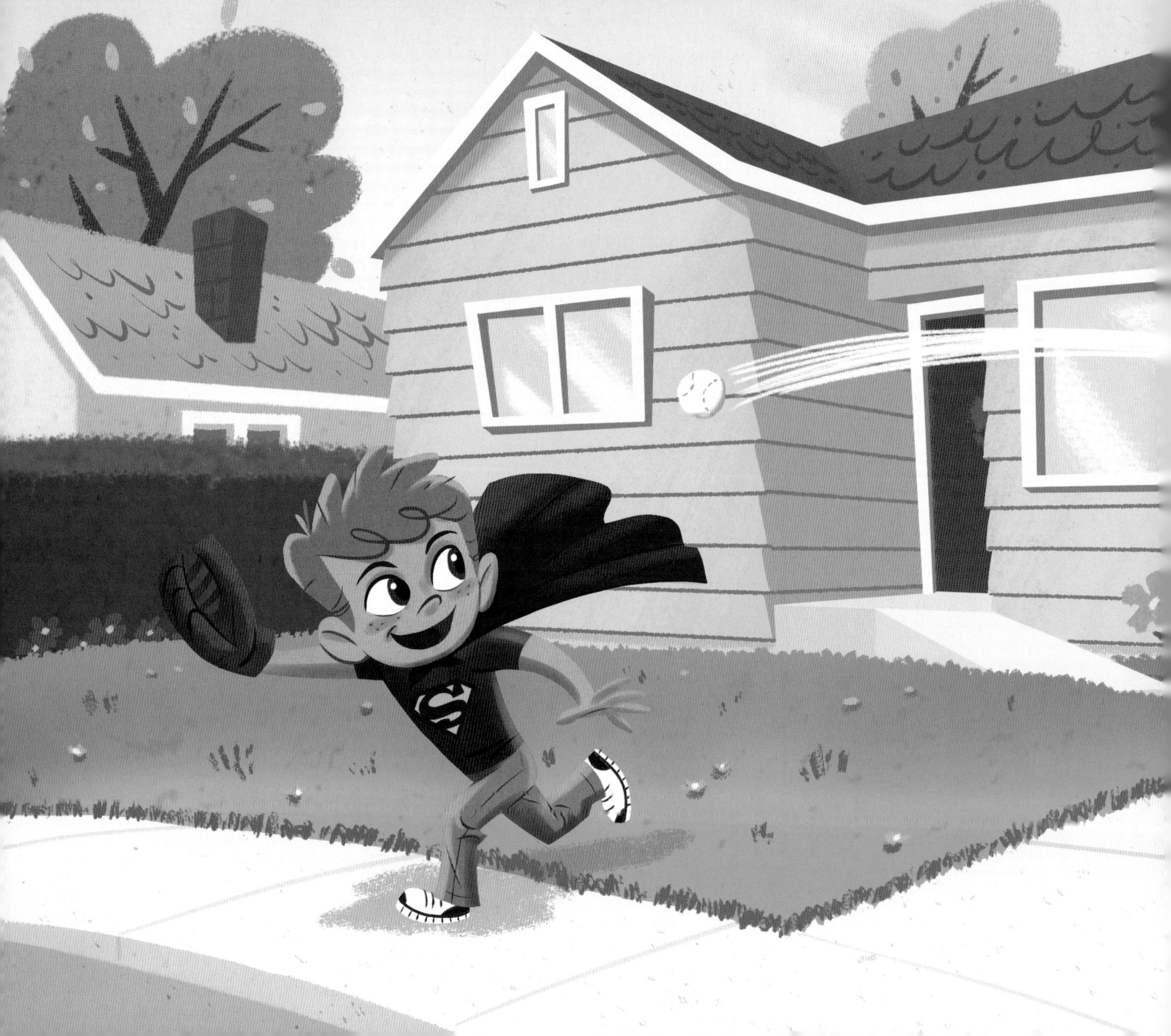

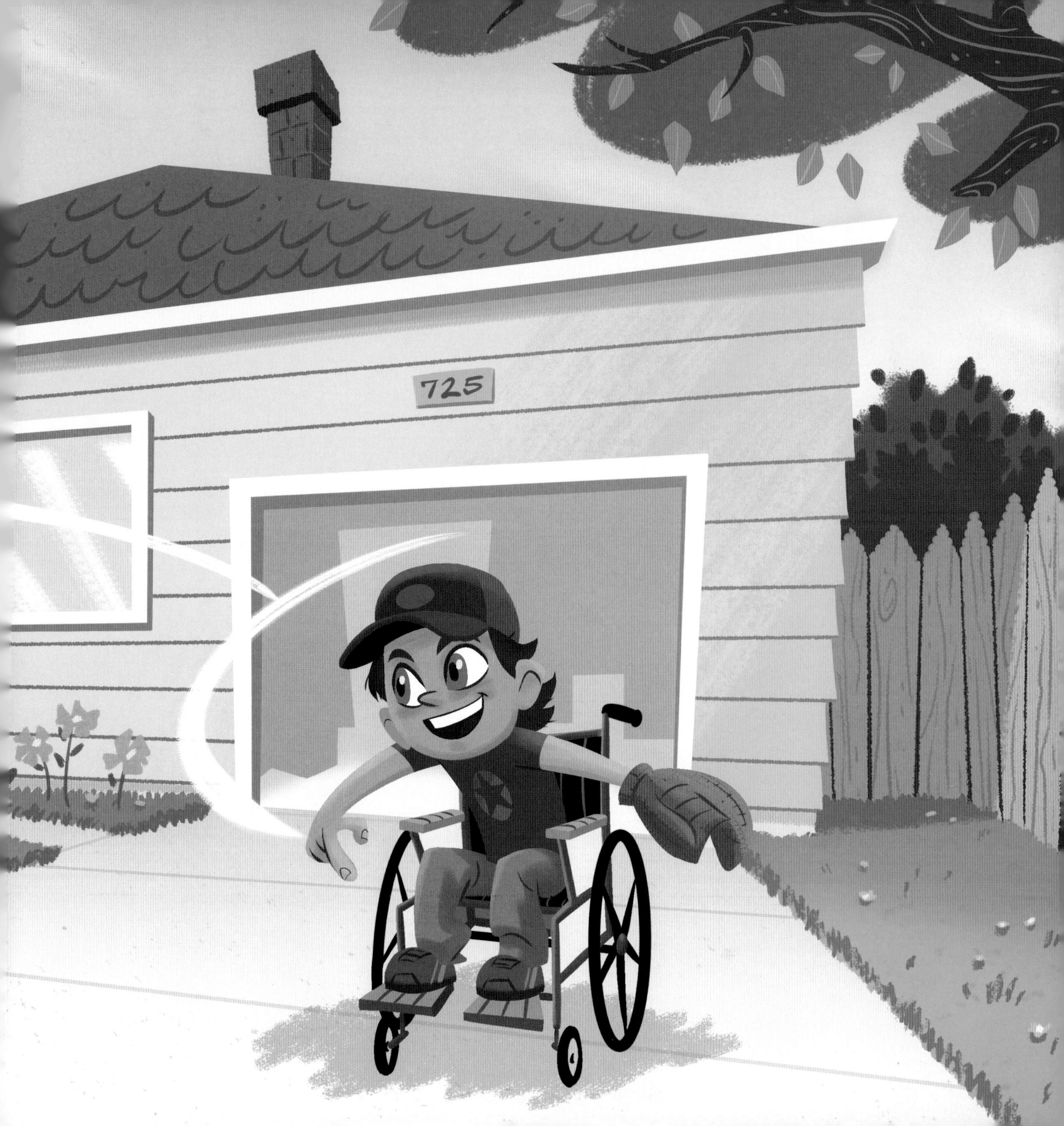
725

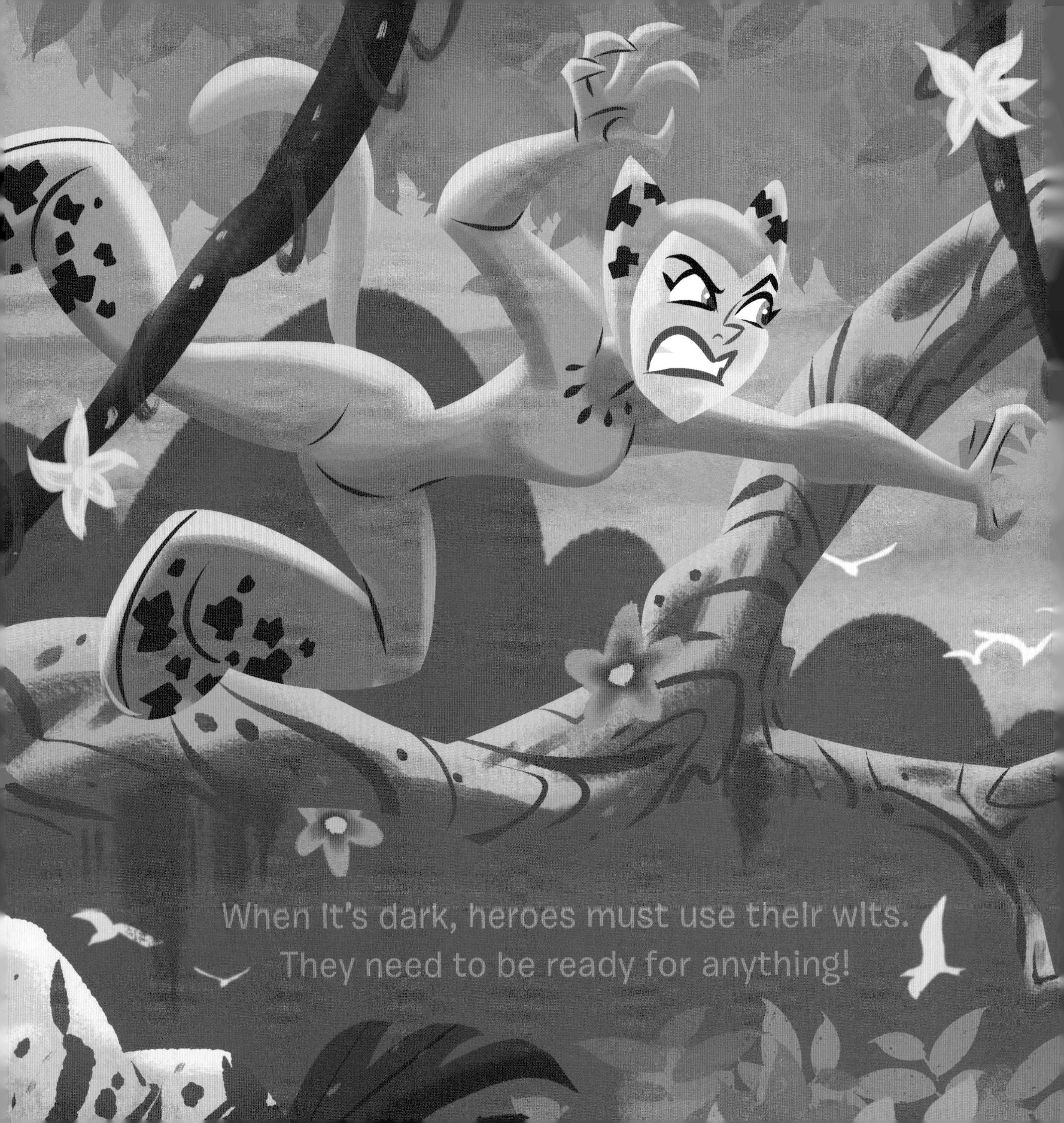

When it's dark, heroes must use their wits.
They need to be ready for anything!

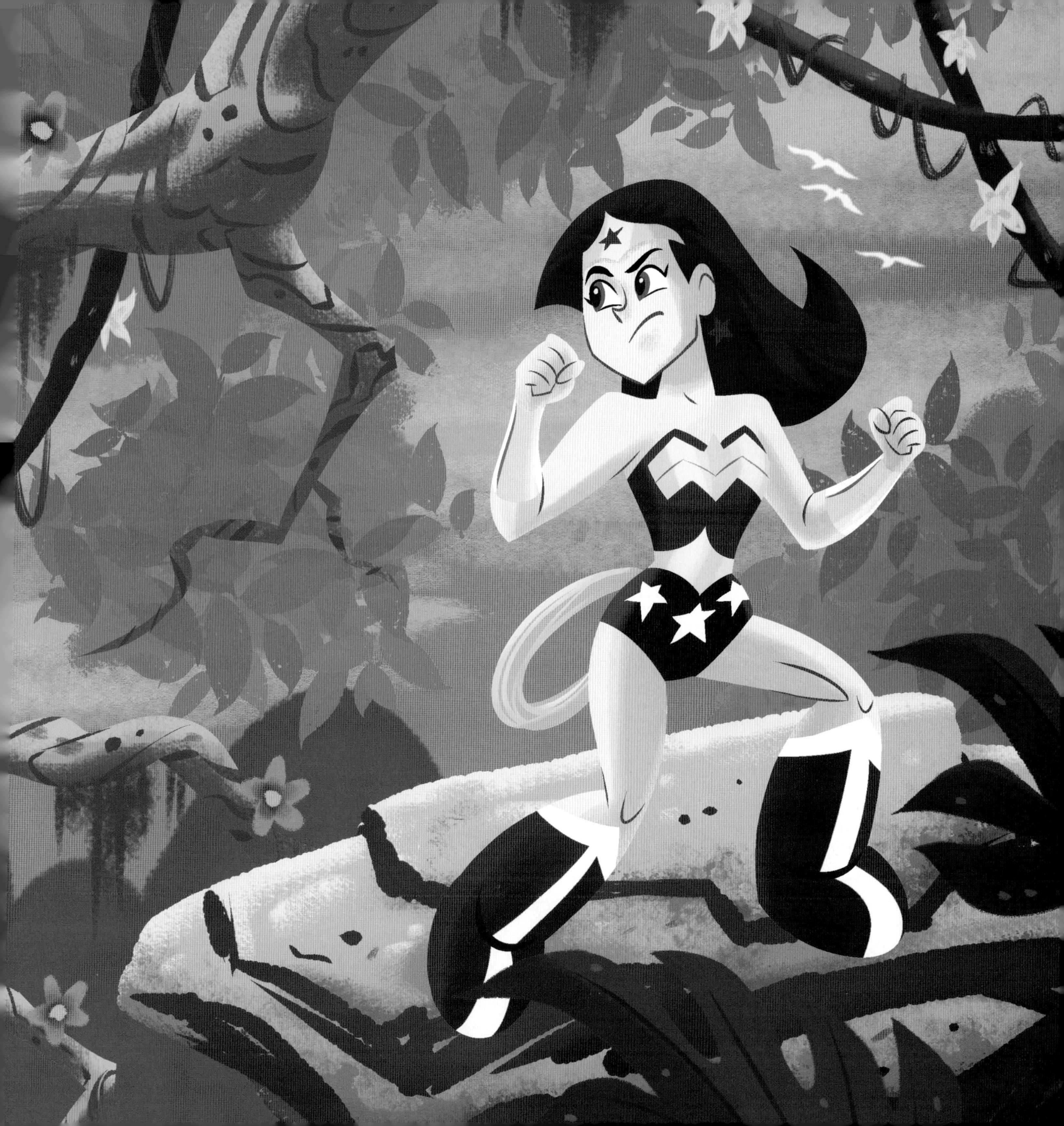

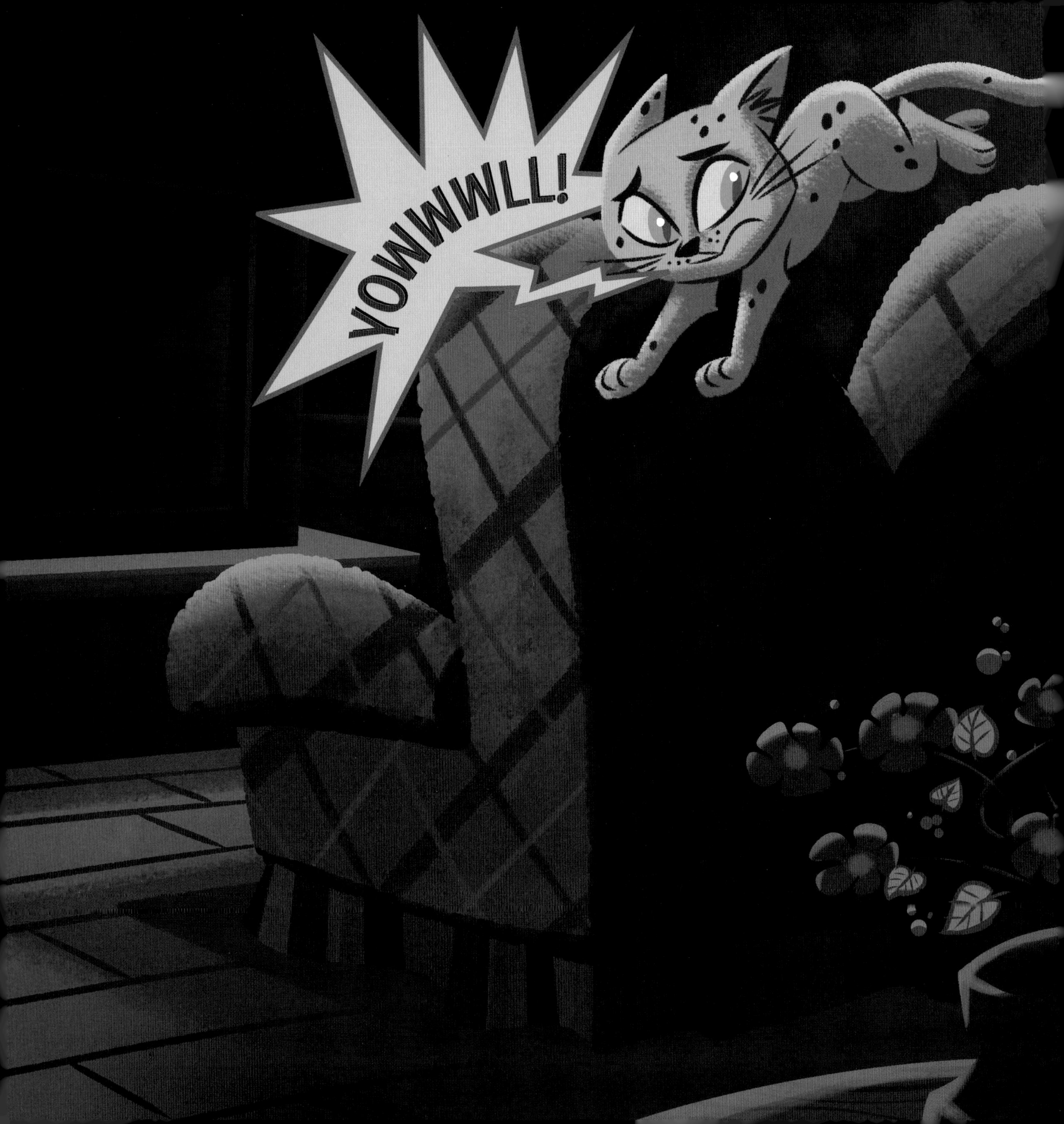
YOWWWLL!

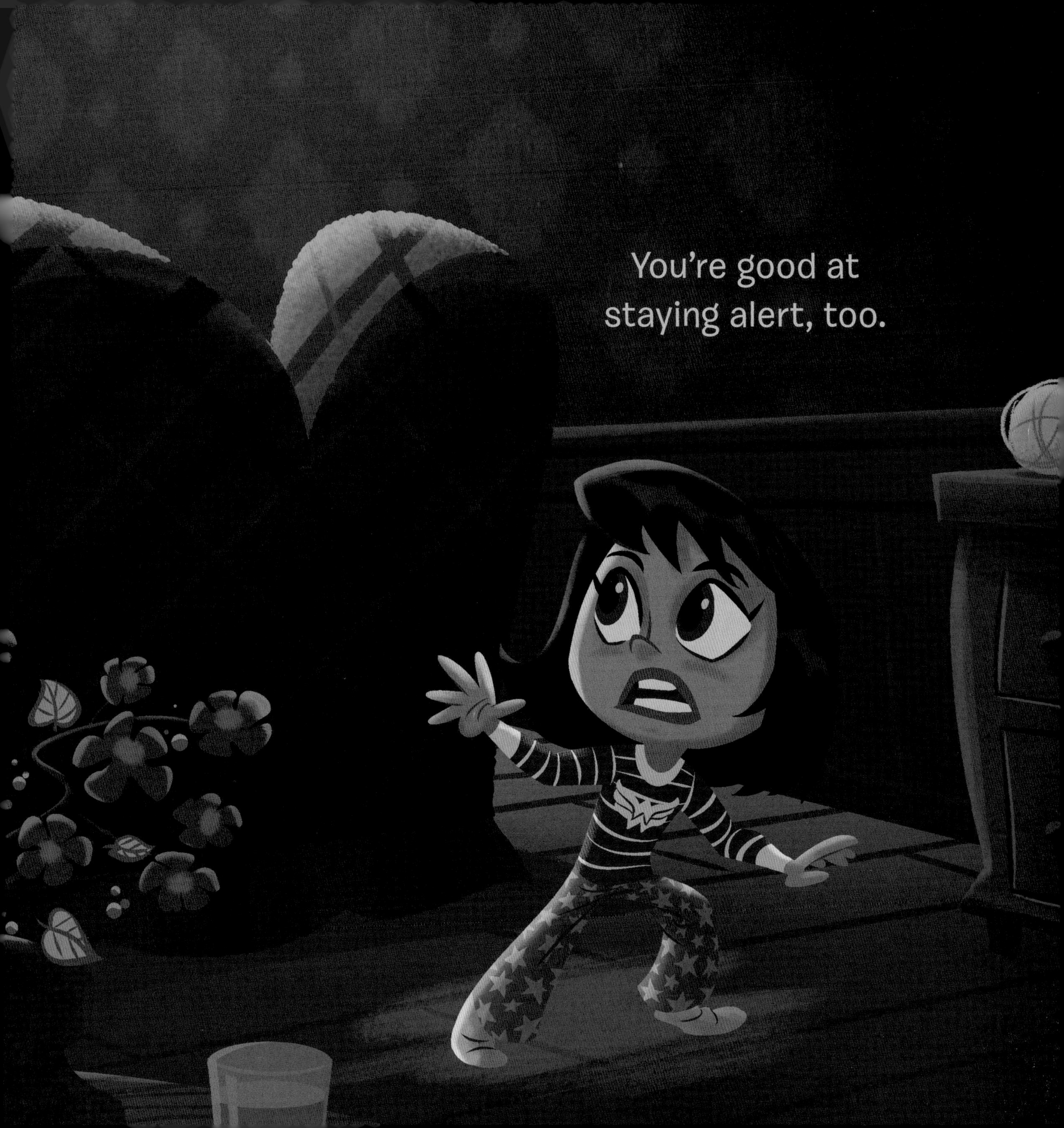

You're good at
staying alert, too.

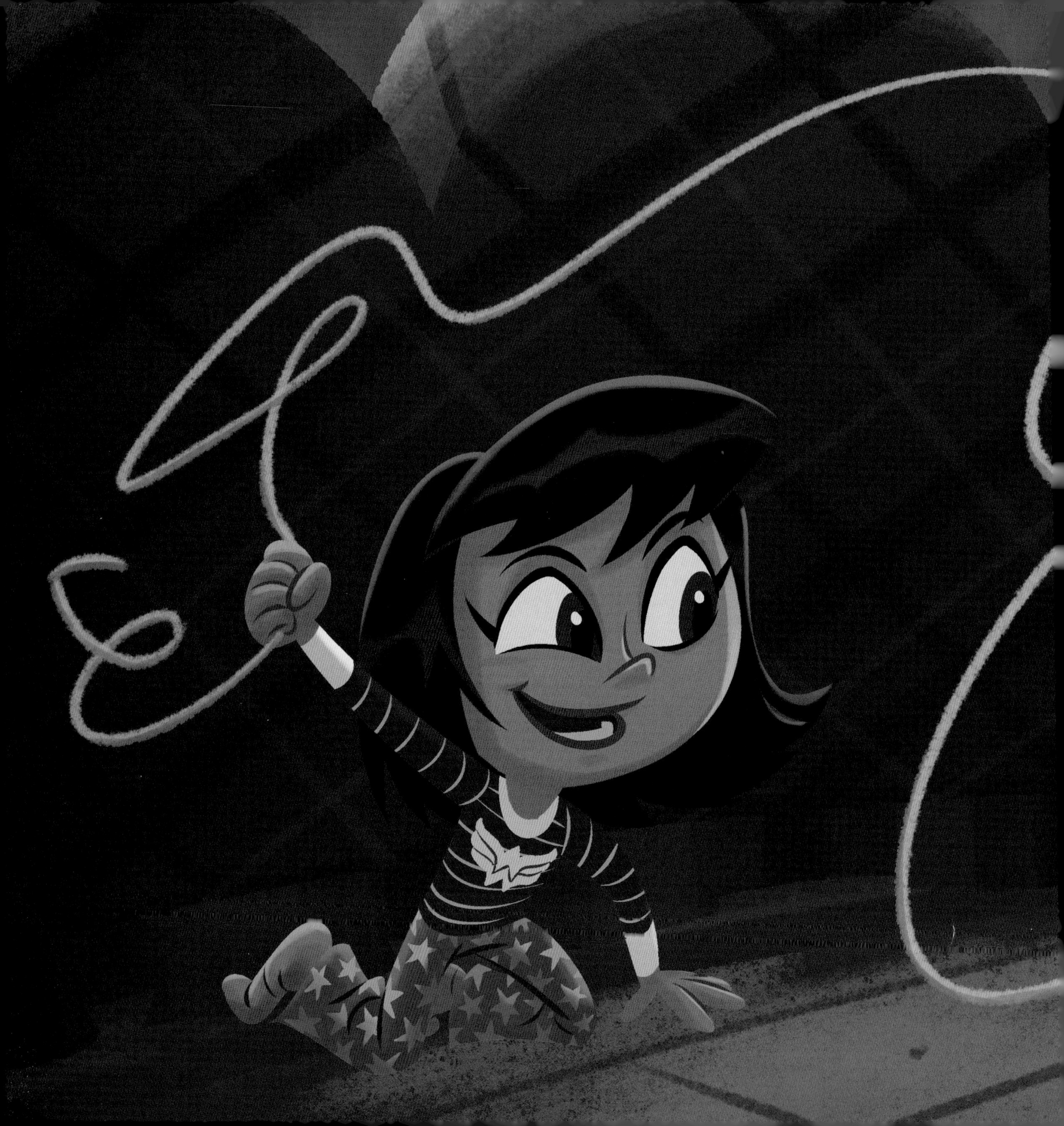

If you get up late at night to use the bathroom, don't let noises surprise you. Maybe your cat just likes to play!

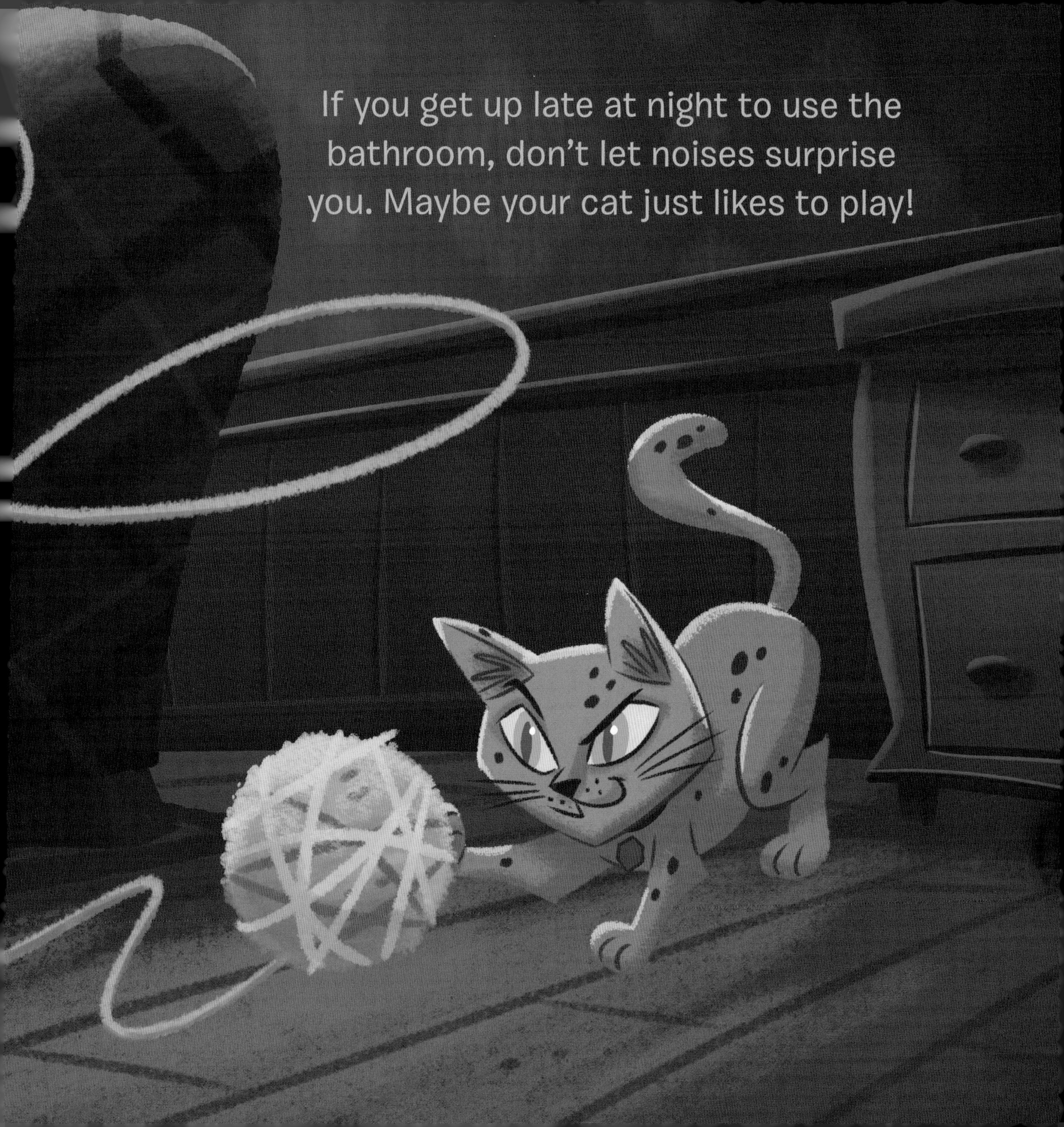

The Super Friends never let fear stop them from doing their jobs.

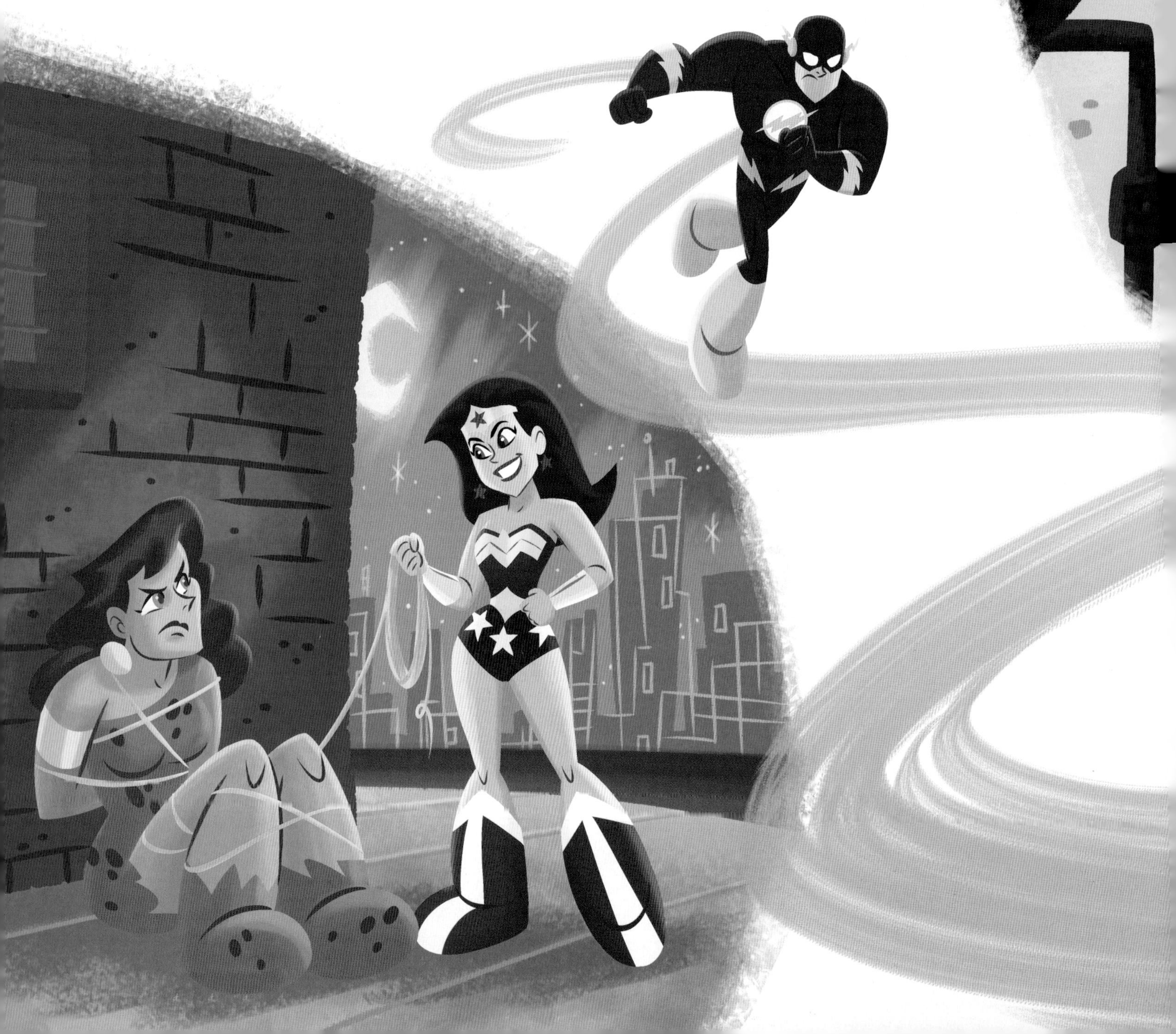

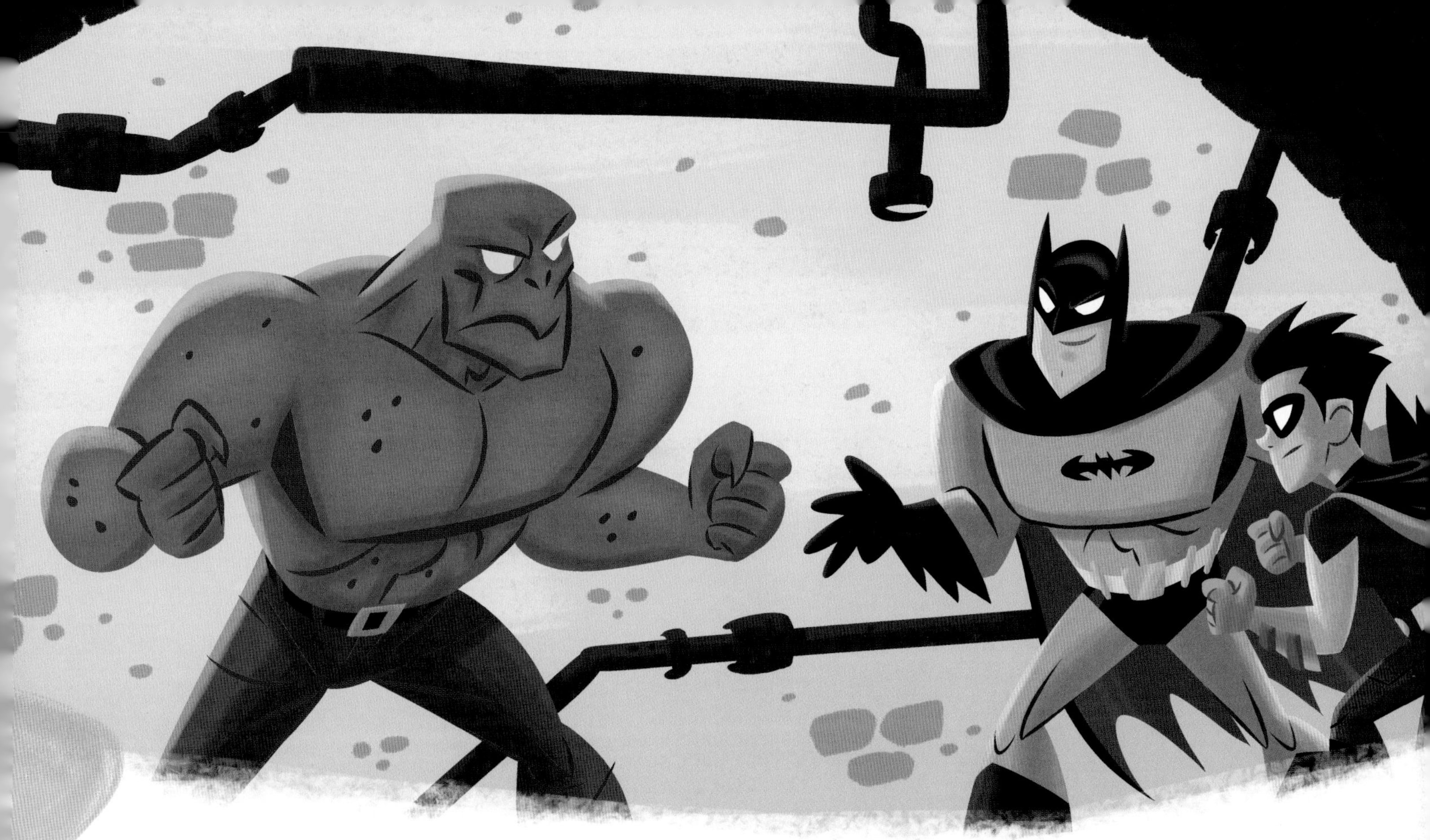

They are true heroes.

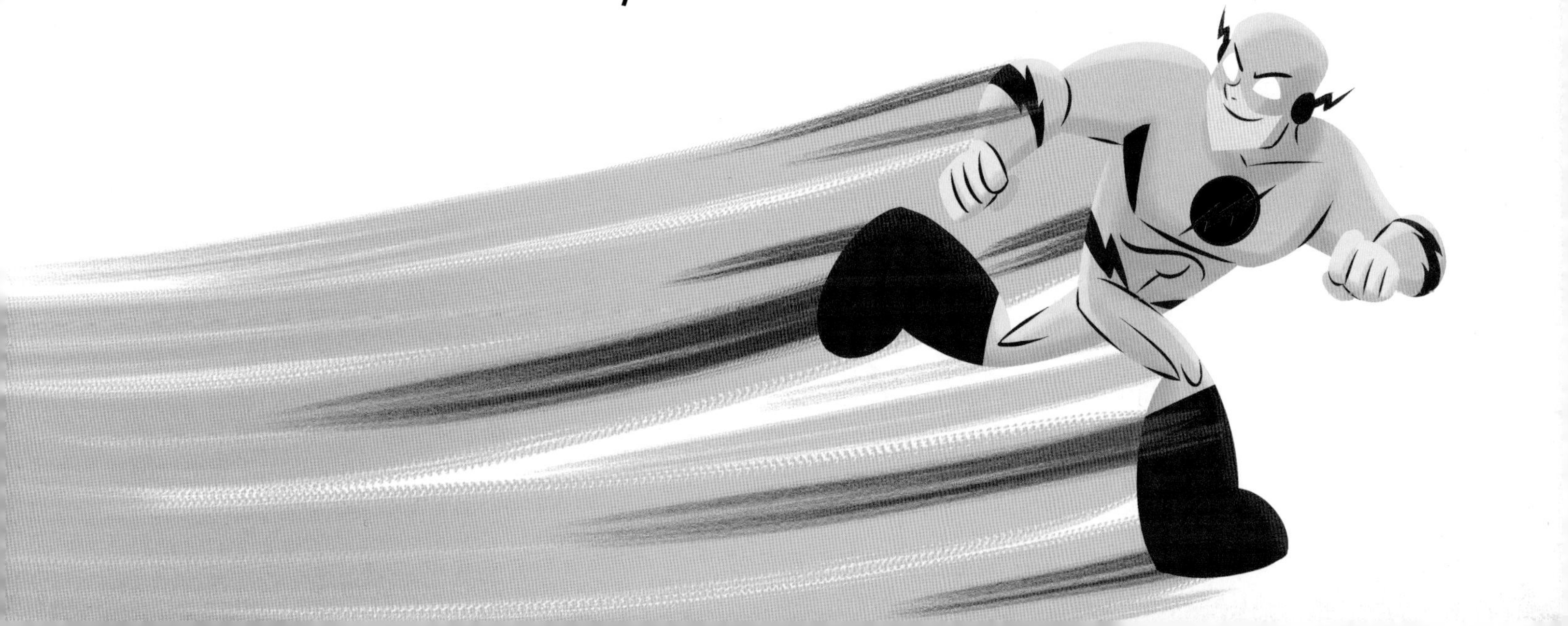

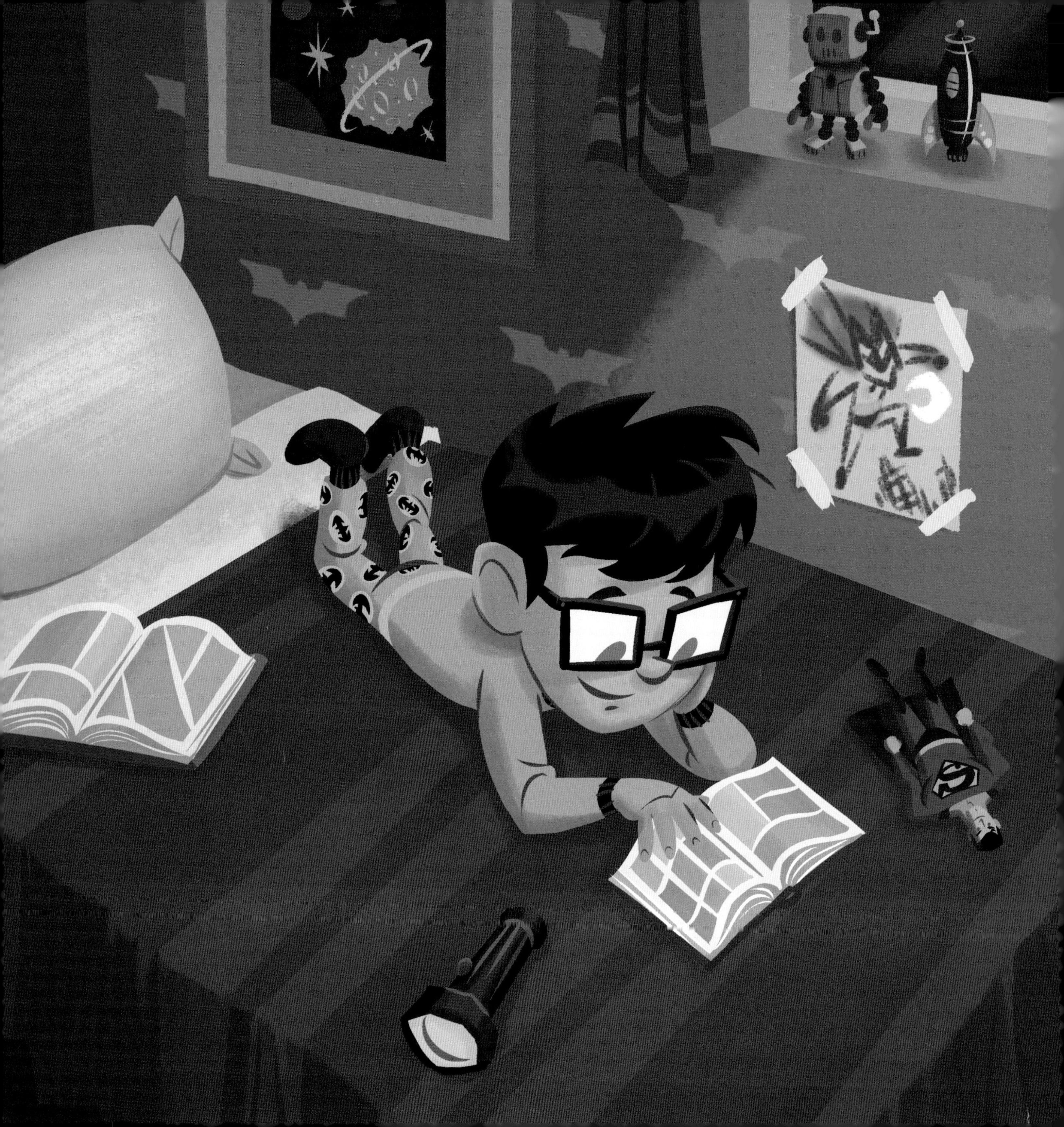

You're a hero, too! You know that
a favorite book, toy, night-light,
or flashlight can help you conquer fear.

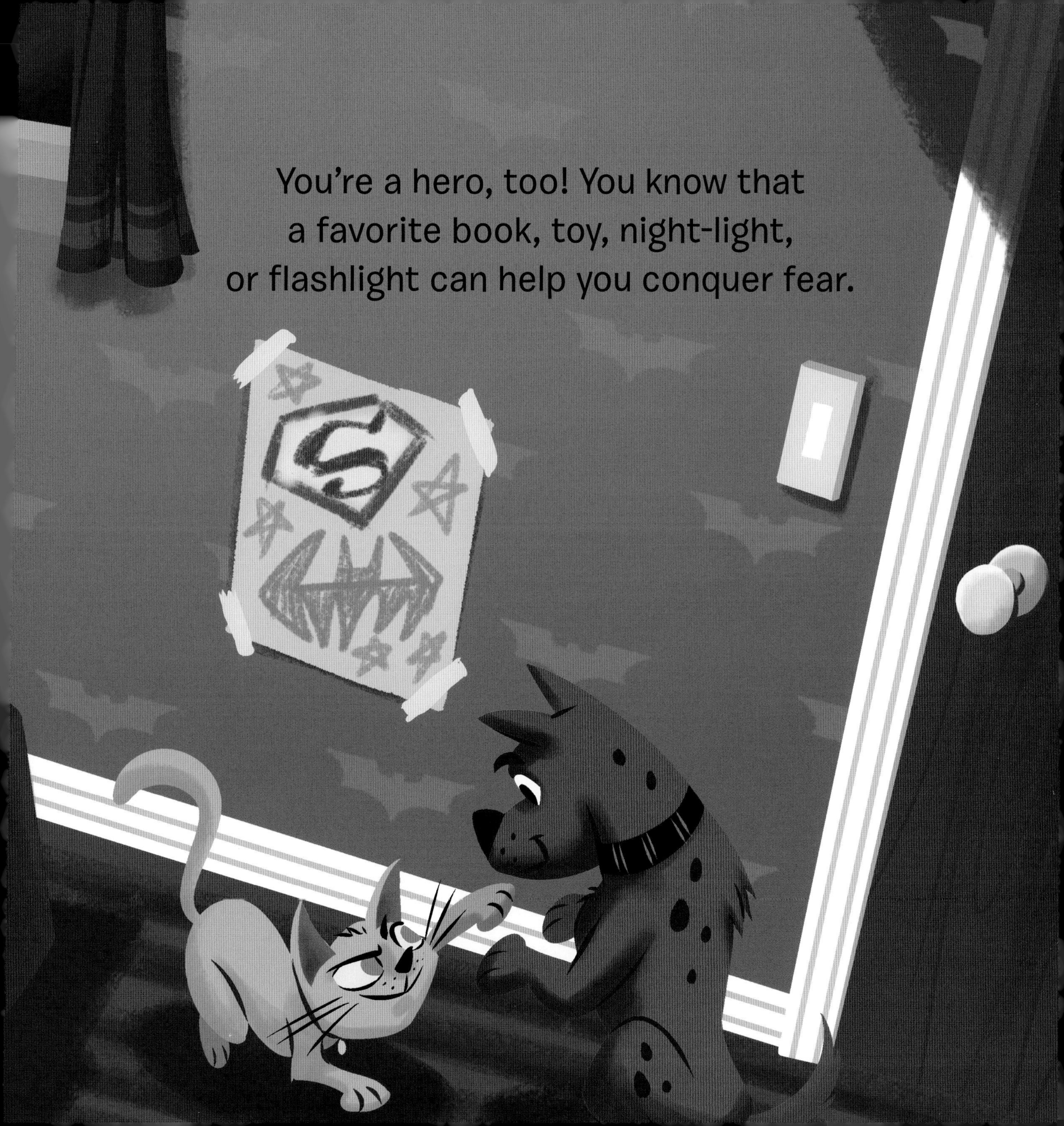

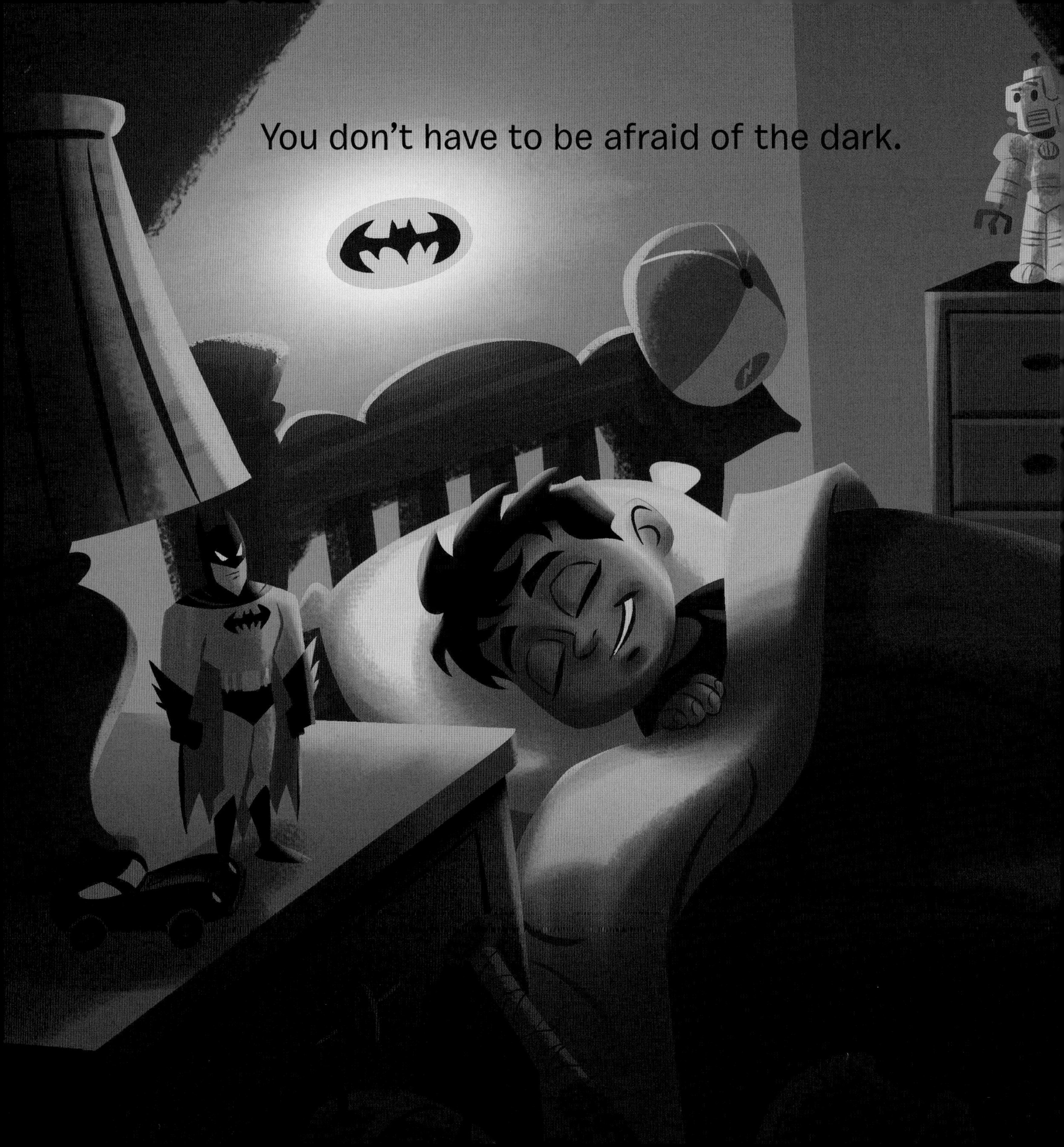

You don’t have to be afraid of the dark.

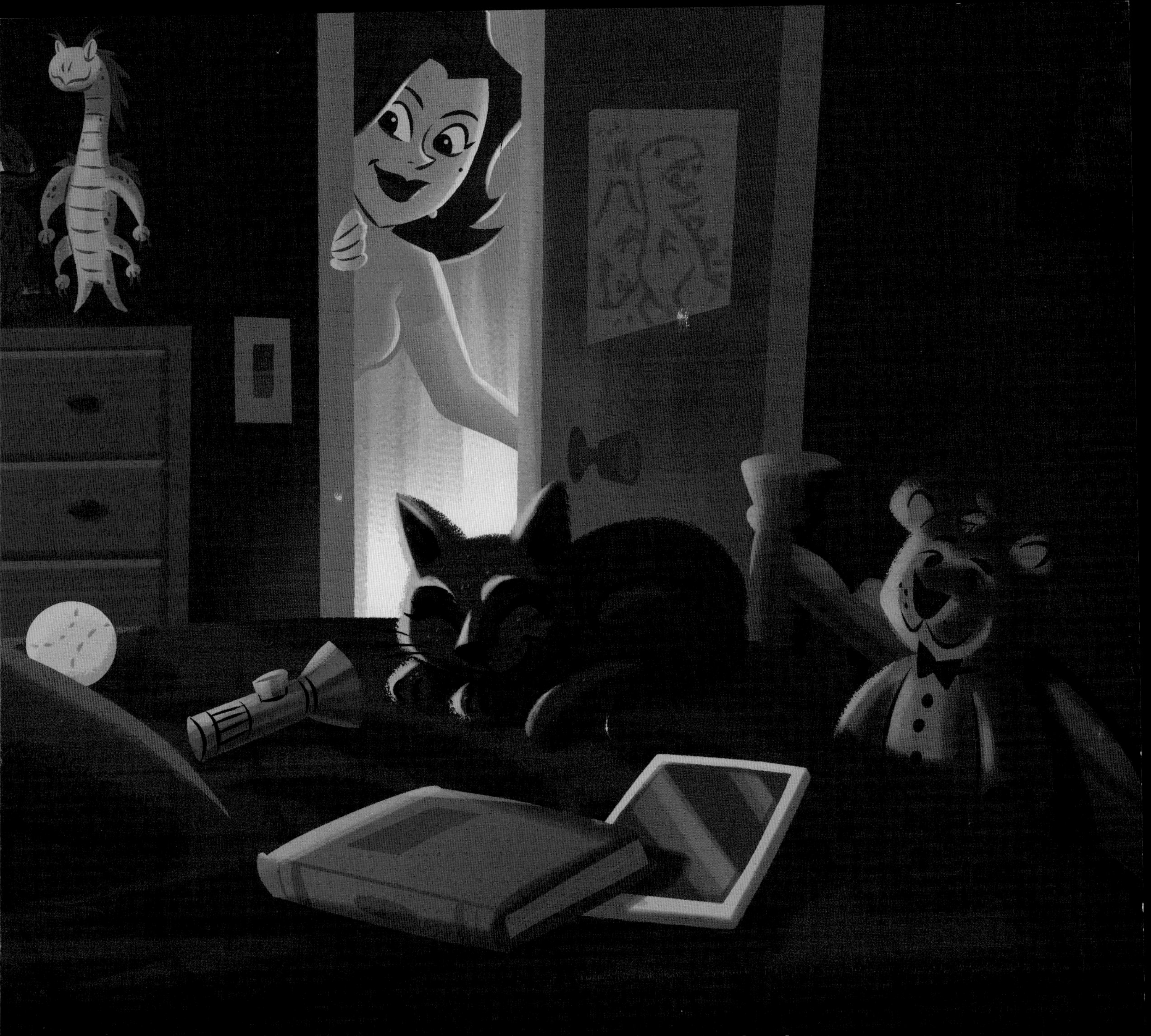

You have all the tools and knowledge you need to be brave . . . just like Batman!

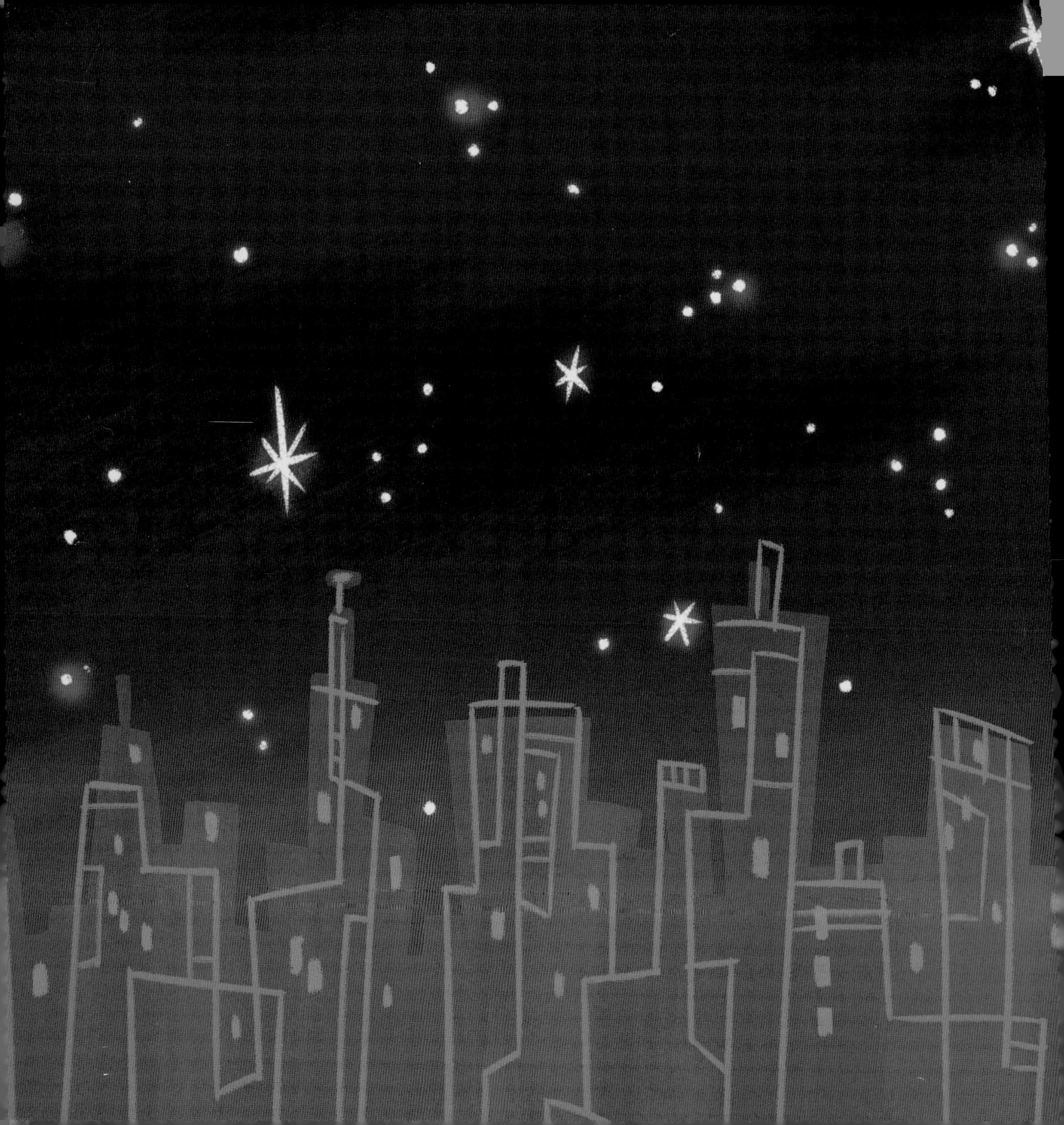